NO. 22
PLEASURE CITY

Guernica World Editions 3

NO. 22 PLEASURE CITY

Mark Fishman

GUERNICA
World
EDITIONS
TORONTO • BUFFALO • LANCASTER (U.K.)
2018

Michael Mirolla, editor
David Moratto, cover design and interior layout
Guernica Editions Inc.
1569 Heritage Way, Oakville, (ON), Canada L6M 2Z7
2250 Military Road, Tonawanda, N.Y. 14150-6000 U.S.A.
www.guernicaeditions.com

Distributors:
University of Toronto Press Distribution,
5201 Dufferin Street, Toronto (ON), Canada M3H 5T8
Gazelle Book Services, White Cross Mills
High Town, Lancaster LA1 4XS U.K.

First edition.
Printed in Canada.

Legal Deposit—First Quarter
Library of Congress Catalog Card Number: 2017960395
Library and Archives Canada Cataloguing in Publication
Fishman, Mark, 1954-, author
No. 22 pleasure city / Mark Fishman. -- First edition.

(Guernica world editions ; 3)
Issued in print and electronic formats.
ISBN 978-1-77183-309-7 (softcover).--ISBN 978-1-77183-310-3 (EPUB).
--ISBN 978-1-77183-311-0 (Kindle).

I. Title. II. Title: Number 22 pleasure city. III. Title: Number
twenty-two pleasure city.

PS3606.I835N6 2018   813'.6   C2017-907298-6   C2017-907299-4

NO. 22
PLEASURE CITY

A reliable witness said that he saw her from an upper-story window and described her as a young woman, maybe thirty, wearing a pair of jeans cut low at the hips and a white short-sleeved shirt that showed her muscular upper arms when the billowing, knee-length beige trench coat blew open and off her shoulders because she was walking so fast. Her navel was pierced by something with a diamond in it and the diamond had winked at him with a reflected ray of sunlight.

She was above-average height and wore low-heeled shoes that clattered as she walked along the sidewalk beneath the overhanging branches of trees, and what had drawn him to the window in the first place was the mouth-watering racket of her footsteps echoing in the street. He went directly to the window whenever he heard a woman's footsteps because he liked to watch them as they walked. He said that this woman's walk was something special. She was slender and her hips swayed noticeably but unselfconsciously, with confidence and purpose. In his opinion, she was going somewhere in a hurry.

Nothing much moved along the streets of the Midwestern city in the region of the Great Lakes early in the morning, and anything that did move, whether human or machine, went about it at a crawl. Everyone and everything but Angela Mason. She walked determinedly along the sidewalk on Prospect Avenue toward the intersection without seeing more than a few passing cars, a couple of city buses and taxis, and one or two bicycles. She waited impatiently at the signal until the small figure changed its position and its color from red to green like someone walking and going nowhere. She smiled, then crossed the intersection, hesitating for a second in the middle to look to the left and right.

She went on her way with long strides, her shoes clattering on the sidewalk. A gulp came to her throat. She wanted to slip unobtrusively into a crowd but there was no sign of one. A handsome man came toward her, and as he came closer she saw that he was wincing. An unlit cigarette hung down from his lips, and it jerked up with each grimace. He lit it, and the lighted match stayed lit. She sized him up. He tried to smile for her, but only one side of his mouth could manage it. He dropped the match and walked past her.

There were a few other passersby, but they didn't look at her for more than the time it took to make sure they didn't collide with someone else. Angela felt that someone was following her, or that someone coming her way or fading out behind her back was watching her. She looked around several times before arriving at the next intersection. She checked the time on her wristwatch. She turned right at Edgewater, walked a block, turned right on Wilson Drive and nearly ran into a woman riding a bicycle on the sidewalk. The bicycle swerved at the last second and she jumped to the edge of the sidewalk to the grass and came to a halt just in front of a wooden bench painted green.

She was trembling. She clenched her fists so tightly that her knuckles were pale. She licked her lips, telling herself her tongue felt like a dried-out sponge. She swallowed, then rubbed the salivary glands under her chin to make them work. Now she moistened her lips with her tongue. She sat down on the bench, facing the flow of traffic and the lake.

She raised her hand and mechanically began to stroke her hair. She gave the street a steady look. A car pulled off Wilson Drive half-way onto the curb. Her eyes opened wide. Then she felt a hand press firmly down on her shoulder. She didn't jump. She turned her head slowly, craning her neck. A face she didn't know looked mildly down at her. The eyes in it shone with a peculiar light that didn't come from sunlight. A hand squeezed her upper arm. She felt something like a pinprick at the base of her neck. She looked straight ahead and smiled sweetly, her eyelashes fluttered, and she got up from the bench. She didn't need any help, but she let herself be guided toward a waiting car. The rear door opened. A hand gave her a gentle push from behind, she ducked her head, and another hand came to rest on top of her head to protect it from striking the roof. She slid across the seat. The man got in beside her and shut the door. The car pulled leisurely away from the curb.

At first her face was stiff like a mask. Then she felt a warm, enveloping glow that spread from her neck downward and played between her legs. The tension in her body was completely gone. She relaxed, letting her mind become pleasantly blank. She turned her head, following traffic that seemed to move in slow motion past the window, each car, bus and taxi making its way in the steady flow on the street.

The landscape changed slowly in front of her bleary eyes. Thinking was difficult, her ability to concentrate was so light, and it didn't matter that she could not get her floating thoughts down properly. They were up there somewhere like helium balloons. She tugged gently on the strings to bring them down. They didn't respond. Only the slight quivering of her fingers revealed that there was still some energy left in her.

Burt Pohl didn't wait for the elevator. He climbed the stairs in a rush, two at a time, without losing his balance, until he got to the fifth floor. He fumbled with the statue in the niche, found the latch-key she kept under it. His fingers held the key nervously. He stood in front of Angela's door knowing what he was doing there and knowing that he shouldn't be doing what he was going to do because it wasn't like him to barge in on her except that now he had no choice and was compelled by an urgency set in motion by fear. But what that fear was all about he didn't know. Bad luck stood right next to him.

The key fit the lock and he turned the doorknob and eased the door open. He smelled something sickly sweet and thick in the air the minute he let himself in and shut the door behind him.

He flattened himself against the wall, the key held loosely in his hand. It was dark where he stood, listening. At first the silence was so deep that it hummed in his ears. A light shone from the adjacent room. He took a long breath and stepped away from the wall. He crouched tensely, alert for the slightest sound. Then a low voice in the next room rasped out what sounded like an order. He stood up and groped along the wall for a light switch. A fan of deep-blue rays of light streamed out of the next room. He didn't find a light switch.

Pohl took a step forward. The deep-blue light changed to a warm, yellow light. He heard heavy breathing. A man's low voice went on giving orders that sounded more like instructions, not an aggressive voice, but authoritative. Pohl went dead-slow to the half-open door of the adjacent room, pushed it noiselessly aside, and peered in. It was Angela's living room, he'd been here a dozen times, but it didn't look at all like the same room.

Angela crouched in a corner with her back against the wall. She wore a black sleeveless T-shirt and panties. Her skin glistened with sweat in the buff light. Pohl had never seen her like this. Her mouth was forced open and her lips drawn back by a medium-sized ball held in place by a strap that went around her head, pinning her hair against her ears. Her arms were bent awkwardly behind her. He couldn't see if they were tied up.

She tilted her head backward, touching the wall. Her eyes reflected the yellowish light. In this position, her knees pointed straight out in front of her. Pohl's gaze went from her knees to her inner thighs. Her panties were pulled aside by something sticking out of her pussy. He could hear a low, humming sound that came from the thing inside her. It was kept there by her evenly-distributed weight and the object's contact with the floor. He squinted. Angela moved mechanically a few inches up and down on it. Her feet were splayed. She rode the vibrator with her eyes partly shut. A moan came from her throat.

Pohl turned his head away and saw a man standing on the opposite side of the room, watching Angela. He couldn't see the features of the man's face, the light was behind him, but it was the silhouette of a man wearing a neat, dark suit. He stood with his legs apart and his feet firmly planted on the floor, his hands lost in the pockets of his trousers. Then his voice came out in a gasp. "That's enough," he said. "Now, come here."

Angela went willingly. She pushed off the wall with the back of her head, she edged forward on her knees. Her distorted mouth, a wide, perverted grin, pleased the observing man. A squeaking noise came from her bare knees moving across the polished floor. The man stepped out of the light to let the full force of it wash over her. She was more breathtaking now than any other time Pohl had seen her. He quickly forgot about the other man and spent a long time looking at the woman he loved.

The man in the neat, dark suit sneezed, then wiped his nose with a handkerchief. Pohl's eyes snapped off Angela and switched to the man. But there was still a humming sound coming from the thing inside her, the muscles held it snugly in place, and he turned his head again to look at her. She strained her neck and her head and body went from side to side as she advanced toward the man. A thread of saliva hung from the corner of her mouth. It swung outward, then attached itself to her chin and hung down from there. Pohl liked the look of it.

Angela lost her balance. She fell over on her side, her face turned toward Pohl. The strap of the ball-gag came loose and the ball, wet and shiny, popped out of her mouth when she hit the floor. Her hands weren't tied behind her back, she'd just kept them there obediently. She didn't see Pohl. She started to laugh, the laughter built into a roar, and the man giggled like a twelve-year-old girl. It was the sort of laugh that made Pohl bite his lower lip. He didn't like it, and he didn't like the man who didn't try to stifle it because it was really painful to see Angela doing what she was doing with a man who laughed like that. He groaned, let the latchkey fall from his hand. It made a light ringing sound on the floor that got Angela's attention. She raised her head, saw him, and her eyes blinked, startled. Her hands went forward, bracing herself to stand up. The vibrator fell out of her pussy and spun in circles on the floor. Pohl turned, ran out of the apartment. He took the stairs two at a time, going down.

Lew Burnett pulled on his trousers over a pair of silk socks, tucked in his shirt, fastened his belt, and tied the knot of his tie with an expression on his face that suggested the tie was going to be used to hang him. Angela wanted something from him and he didn't know what it was going to be. She wouldn't have said yes to what she'd been saying no to for so long if she didn't want to get something out of him. He picked out a pair of low, black leather boots. He cleaned them with a soft cloth and a horsehair brush, slipped them on and tied them up. He combed his hair straight back and sprayed himself with an earthy scent. He laughed softly. It was the laugh of a twelve-year-old girl. The face in the mirror laughed with him, gave him a generous look and smiled.

He switched off the lights in each room as he made his way to the front door, gathered up his keys, a handful of coins from the entrance table. He made a loose fist around the coins, shook them in his hand like dice. Folding the raincoat over his arm, he went out the door and locked it behind him.

Twenty minutes later he pulled over to the curb on Birch Street and cut the engine. He sat behind the wheel thinking although he knew that thinking wasn't going to give him any clue what she was up to. But he knew what he was going to do with her. He figured that she didn't have any experience with what he wanted from her. Doing it with a kind of amateur made it more exciting. He felt the blood pulse in his veins. He stared through the light rain sprinkling the windshield at the entrance to Angela's building on Lake Street. No matter what she wanted from him it was going to be worth it. The thought of her doing what he told her to do enveloped him like a warm bath, and he lounged back in the leather upholstered seat and allowed the undulating waters to cover him.

He lit a cigarette and watched the smoke swirl up and out and break like a wave against the dashboard. When he finished the cigarette he tossed it out the window. Burnett looked at himself in the rearview mirror, put the tip of his finger in his mouth, moistened it, then reached up to smooth his eyebrows. He got out of the car with the raincoat in his hand.

A quarter moon rode high over the buildings of the downtown district sliced down the middle by a black river faintly colored by pale moonlight and spanned by bridges lit by sodium-vapor lamps. Rows of streetlights stretched off in all directions, and to the southeast, parts of the surface of the 22,400-square-mile lake shrugged its white-capped shoulders in gusts of wind.

Clouds gathered in the sky above the lake and it looked like rain. They moved slowly in from the north, becoming thick and dark, traveling low and grazing the tops of tall buildings, and in a little while a mistlike rain blew between the buildings.

The streetlights and neon signs on Jackson Street made crazy swirling patterns of color on the sidewalk and the roofs and hoods and windshields of cars parked the length of the street. Then the rain began to fall in sheets, flattening discarded newspapers against the sides of buildings and on the sidewalk. The wind blew plastic cups and empty beer and soda cans in the gutter, making a racket with the sound of bouncing hollow aluminum containers, a racket almost but not quite drowned out by the steady pounding of the downpour.

The wind died down but the rain fell continuously all over the night city: on the brick façade of the huge brewery where a nightshift was working, a disused appliance manufacturer at the edge of the city limit and a suburb, the expensive apartment buildings overlooking the lake on the Eastside, a tool and die factory, a tractor assembly plant, the taverns and modest dirty, cream-colored brick houses on the Southside, the warehouses along the river where all the windows had been dark for hours, and the wealthy suburban areas to the north and east.

The rain began to slacken, and a heavy silence filled the vacancy the rain had left in the city.

Angela pressed the button next to the intercom to let Lew Burnett into the building. She was thirty years old. She wore a short black skirt and an emerald silk blouse. Her pale skin was as smooth as the skin of an eighteen-year-old. Her reddish-brown hair was cut at a slight angle to her shoulders. She swung the door open with enthusiasm. Burnett walked in wet with a raincoat over his arm. She started to say something, but stopped herself at the moment he turned to look at her. Her hands were a delicate gesture, and her sea-blue eyes were like the sun on a lake.

He handed her his raincoat, then went straight to the living room, sat down in a chair, threw one leg over the other, dangling a boot that kicked out gently at the air. She went to the bathroom and came back with a towel. She handed it to him. He rubbed his hair with it, then combed his hair back with his hands. Angela slanted her eyes down at him and the smile on her mouth was the way he wanted a woman to smile at him. He giggled. She turned around and went out of the room. He stood up, looking at the furniture, walls and floor. Angela came back an instant later. Burnett looked up, glanced around from wall to wall, then the ceiling again and then the floor.

Angela had her hands on her hips.

Burnett sat down again in the chair.

"Where do we start?" Angela asked, hitching up her skirt as she sat opposite him on the arm of a chair.

He looked at her, then quickly looked away. Something in her eyes told him she might not be the amateur he thought she was. Or that there was something else going on and that it was so far away from him that he'd never find out what it was. "Don't we get something to drink?" he asked confidently, looking at her again.

"Take a good look," she said, moving her hand between her legs and pushing her skirt up. She wasn't wearing anything under her skirt. "Enjoying it?"

Burnett shrugged. He looked away from the sparse red hair between her legs and examined his boots, rubbing his knees vigorously with the palms of his hands, then looked up at her.

"I thought so," she said, straightening her skirt. She left the room to fix them a drink.

Burnett sighed. His eyes wandered to the windows. A few apartments across the street were lit up. An occupant of one of them came into view, a man in his late forties, and he looked out the window at Burnett, and then didn't stop looking at him. Burnett responded by getting up and lowering the blinds in front of each of the windows, then giggled. Angela came back with two glasses of whisky with ice.

She handed him a glass. "To our success, yours and mine," she said, raising the glass out in front of her.

Burnett downed his in a gulp.

"I'll get you another. You look like you need it."

He shook his head, and gazed at the face of his white-gold wristwatch. "No," he said. He looked properly solemn.

"Now, where were we?" Angela said, taking a sip of whisky and fidgeting with the hem of her skirt.

Pohl stood at the service entrance on the Birch Street side of Angela's building a few feet and around the corner from the main entrance on Lake Street, with a handkerchief in his hand, wiping the perspiration from his forehead and breathing hard after coming down five flights of stairs two at a time. He couldn't vomit properly. There was a strand of bitter, greenish bile dangling like a fish line from his mouth.

He went over it in his mind. He saw what he thought he'd seen but he had a hard time accepting it. Angela squirming on a vibrator for a man in a neat dark suit that he didn't know and had never seen before. A man whose head he'd like to kick through the goalposts. He brushed away the strand of bile with the back of his hand, then dried it with the handkerchief. He straightened himself enough to walk without looking like a drunk. He shook his head. Angela crawling on her hands and knees with the thing inside her. The picture hit him hard.

He walked sharp on Birch away from Lake to the corner, turned without looking back, and made his way home, a twenty-minute walk heading southwest, clutching his stomach. A block before he got there, on Jackson Street, he ran into a short, middle-aged man, wearing a lightweight off-white linen suit, smoking a cigar, who wasn't looking where he was going. They collided without mishap, but the man snapped his mouth shut and broke the cigar in two.

"No objection, my fault," the man said.

"I think so," Pohl answered, nodding.

"Sorry. Any idea why?" the man said with a smile.

"Not interested," Pohl said impatiently.

Nausea came up to his throat like a rope from a knot in his belly. Pohl took a forward step and the man didn't move. He took another forward step and the man didn't move and Pohl bumped into him.

He stepped back and tried to walk around him but the man's bulk was a short wall on the sidewalk.

"Let's not play innocent," the man said, grinning.

"Save it. I don't want to know."

"I was just fucking. I'm not thinking about where I'm going because where I've been is more interesting." He tossed his bent cigar into the street.

Angela stood for a long time under the shower because she didn't like the smell of sex when the smell of it was connected to someone like Lew Burnett. She soaped herself and smiled at the method she'd used to trap him into doing what she wanted him to do for her, but she didn't like the price she'd paid even though it wasn't the first time she'd done something like it. She hadn't learned it in any book, it was a natural gift she'd found in herself.

She shut off the flow of water and dried herself with a thick, fluffy towel. She wasn't worried about Pohl, he'd come sniffing around again, because any man who wanted her as much as he wanted her knew what to do about it. She was sure it made her more attractive to him to have seen her like that free of charge. It gave him something to think about in bed.

She would rather have done it with Pohl instead of Burnett, but she wanted something Burnett could give her and Pohl didn't have it to give and that was what made the difference between them. She smiled, drying her milky skin, the texture of flower petals. She looked at herself in the mirror. The woman looking back at her without any clothes on was strictly ethereal perfection.

Angela went to the bedroom and put on a pair of pajamas. It was almost daylight. She threw herself on the bed, lying on her stomach with the pajama trousers bunched up at her knees, and flipped through the pages of a book. She found the bent corner of a page, eyed it, then leafed through the rest of the book until she got to the last page.

The telephone rang. It was Burnett.

"What are you doing?" he asked.

"Why?"

"In bed already?"

"Where else?" she said indifferently. Burnett meant nothing to her. "Enjoy your evening?"

"What do you think?"

"I don't have to think about it."

"Well, I've been thinking."

"Don't. Just do what I asked you to do. The way I explained it to you. Make yourself useful, I'll let you wear my underwear." She laughed. "Don't complicate things by trying to use your head."

Burnett sighed heavily. "Okay, goodbye."

Angela switched off the light. Her head fell gently to the pillow. She shut her eyes.

The telephone rang again. She frowned. She picked up the receiver. It was Pohl. It couldn't have been anyone else but him. He didn't say a word, just a repeated soft, choking sound, a kind of sob, and the line went dead.

Burnett didn't sleep but his eyes were shut. Why would he go to sleep when he was waiting for the morning sunlight to creep in through the blinds so that he could get out of bed? He thought about Angela, and at the same time he thought that he ought to do something to keep his mind off her, but nothing he came up with worked, and anything he thought about just made him more conscious of the fact that he was trying not to think about her. What he was going to do when he got out of bed had everything to do with Angela. He'd agreed to help her pull off some stunt by looking for a deserted building, a run-down apartment house, a small two-storied shack, an empty Polish flat, a place in Pigsville, it didn't matter, and then getting the information to her in trade for sex, and it was the kind of sex he liked so he was hooked.

He sat up and swung his legs over the side of the bed, pulled a pack of cigarettes from the night table drawer, jabbed one between his tightened lips and struck a match. He leaned back against the mashed feather pillows, gazing at nothing and taking deep drags off the cigarette. His eyes focused on the smoke coming slowly out of his mouth. Burnett put the cigarette out.

In the kitchen he poured himself a glass of orange juice. He looked down at his bare feet and wiggled his toes. The linoleum was cool. Sunlight streamed in through the kitchen window. He hadn't spent much time in the apartment since the last time the housekeeper cleaned it. The appliances gleamed, and he bent his knees to catch a glimpse of his unsteady reflection in the Inox refrigerator door. I'm all there, but I'm only half with it, he told himself. He got hard just thinking of Angela.

He took the glass of orange juice with him to the mirror in the hallway. There were bags under his eyes. He wasn't used to seeing himself like this. After only one night the thing with Angela was already taking its toll.

When he'd finished his coffee, Burnett shaved and showered and dressed himself in another expensive suit. In the study, he telephoned a real estate consultant and asked her for detailed sheets on lots for sale and vacant buildings and remodeling jobs. He gave her a general idea which parts of the city interested him. The consultant promised that the information would be delivered to him by courier at noon.

Burnett wanted to push Angela's plan forward in a hurry. He put the phone down, thought about the prize for finding the right location for her, the place she wanted for whatever reason she wanted it. He shut his eyes. He saw Angela taking off her panties, sliding them down her legs and handing them to him. The scent of her sex was in his nose and he felt the slippery soft fabric against his face. It made him shiver.

Burt Pohl sat in front of the telephone without moving. He was like a statue, his face something carved from rock, a profile of hardened whiteness that hadn't changed since he saw Angela on her hands and knees with a vibrator inside her. The hardship of it had turned his hair half-white and deepened the lines in his face. Maybe that's an exaggeration, but it's killing me. Maybe I want it with her. His eyes were tightly shut and his fingers pressed against his temples. He wanted to talk to her, but he'd choked up when he heard her voice. He lifted the receiver again, punched the numbers. He listened to the ringing at the other end of the line. She didn't answer.

He let the phone ring for a long time, then hung up. He wasn't in a hurry to find out anything that might hurt him more than the hurt he felt from wanting her. He shook his head and got up, started toward the bathroom, shuffling his feet, and the telephone rang. He jerked backward, nearly tripped over the chair. Pohl lifted the receiver.

"Don't you think it's about time you put your clothes on?"

He knew the voice, but he couldn't put a finger on it because his mind was so far away the voice just didn't register until it went on with a few more words that made him smile.

"Or haven't you got anything better to do than waltz around in your pajamas?"

Pohl laughed. It was Shimura, his friend and a detective with the Kawamura Agency.

"Waltzing? Do you know what time it is? It's nine o'clock. Why shouldn't I waltz?" he said, grinning and passing his hand over his head.

"Listen, I'm not working until tomorrow night," Shimura said. "Let's have a drink and something to eat."

Pohl's mind suddenly went blank. He was staring at a picture of Angela that stood in a frame on the table next to him. A tear dribbled out of the corner of his eye. His heart was pounding. He made an effort to pull himself together.

He was glad to hear Shimura's voice, but he was looking and couldn't find anything to say. Pohl let out a sigh.

"Maybe you want to talk about something," Shimura said with a reassuring tone in his voice. "Whatever it is, you haven't done anything wrong."

"Why say that?"

"I can hear it in your voice. It's just plain misery, that's all."

Pohl heaved a great sigh, then found it difficult to catch his breath. At last he said: "Tonight. Eight o'clock. At the Casino Club." He paused. "You're right, I want to talk to you."

"Eight o'clock," Shimura repeated. "We'll figure it out. See you tonight."

"Right."

Shimura hung up.

The receiver buzzed in Pohl's hand, he winced, then blinked several times because he was worn out. He put the phone down, wiped his tear-stained face with the back of his hand, made his way to the bathroom where he turned on the faucet to run a bath, took off his pajamas and folded them neatly, putting them on a shelf. He got into the bathtub with his socks on.

Angela folded her arms across her chest and looked up at the ceiling. A fan spun almost silently in the flower shop, the air barely stirred. Outside, the pale blue spring sky teemed with soft clouds that reached out far above the lake. Cars traveled up and down Prospect Avenue on the Eastside. The leaves of the trees lining the street fluttered in an unseasonably warm, gentle breeze.

There was a coffeehouse next door to the florist. A group of students from the nearby university walked along the sidewalk in front of it, each in turn looking through the plate-glass window at Angela as they trailed sluggishly one after the other into the coffeehouse.

Angela picked out two orchid plants. She waited for the florist and his assistant to finish wrapping the one she was sending to Pohl. She gave them Pohl's address, paid, took the other plant in her arms, and marched out of the shop. A red Dodge pickup slowed down and the driver stared at Angela walking with the orchid in her arms. She raised her eyebrows at the driver. Her distrust of men alternated with her need for them. She gave the driver a smile, but she was thinking of Pohl. She wasn't finished with him. She turned left on Second Street, crossed Lafayette Avenue, turned left on Lake Street, walked to the corner of Birch and Lake.

At five o'clock in the afternoon she got out of the shower and wrapped a towel around herself because the intercom didn't stop buzzing. She'd been on the verge of making herself come as the tide of buzzing knocked her off course. She stuck a slender finger out and pushed the button next to the speaker. It was Burnett.

Burnett left Angela's apartment forty minutes after the meeting he'd sprung on her at five o'clock in the afternoon. He even shook his head at his own stupidity. He wasn't in control of anything with Angela unless she offered the control to him, and most of the time when he thought he had control over anything at all, he was kidding himself. He couldn't get it out of his head. It was the same thing with every woman he had sex with because dominating somebody else amounted to letting himself be dominated. There wasn't any difference. A woman in a tied-up situation was stuck in the same position he was stuck in since his life was permanently bound up in his desires. In spite of that, it was a one-sided exchange with the weight of things leaning heavily in his favor. He might've given her something, let her have a piece of the intimacy, but right from the start he had the door wide open and waiting for him to walk through it, leaving every woman behind.

He walked along the sidewalk past his car trying to put the pieces together and found that the puzzle was already assembled there in front of him. It was the personality he was born with and he'd known for a long time now that he had to go with the current and not try to swim upstream. He felt in his pockets for his cigarettes, put one between his lips and lit it. He took several rapid puffs as his frustration climbed to high gear. When it reached that point he turned around and headed back to the car, threw the cigarette away, got in without switching on the ignition, shut his eyes and rested his head on his wrists with his hands crossed at ten and two on the steering wheel.

By the time he'd taken the elevator to Angela's apartment she had put on a tie wrap satin robe. She stood at the open door, raised her arm and pointed at the living room. Burnett let her go ahead of him. Her unselfconscious stride stirred the knee-length hem, and her narrow hips swayed under the emerald-colored fabric. Spots of water made small, dark blemishes on the back and shoulders of the robe. Her hair was wet.

Angela sat in an armchair with her legs crossed opposite Burnett, the open folds of the robe revealed the muscles of her legs to her upper thighs. It was unbearable. When she uncrossed her legs it was worse. Drops of water glistened just below her knees. Burnett wanted to lick them up, but she caught him staring at her legs and she crossed them again. He asked for a whisky.

She left the room swinging her hips and returned with two glasses of whisky and ice. She put down one of the glasses, then held the robe closed as she leaned forward to hand him his drink. She crossed the room and switched on the CD player with a recording of Orlando Lopez.

She turned to face him. "Well?" she asked.

"I have part of what you want done."

She pulled up a zabuton cushion and sat down at the low table. Burnett sat opposite her in an upholstered straight chair. She looked up at him. The only thing Burnett saw was her bare legs. She straightened the robe, covering her knees with satin.

"Okay, let's see what you've got," she said slowly.

She looked at him. Burnett grinned, thinking of his cock and the rosy flush spreading over the lips of her pussy perfectly out of reach. She ignored the grin. He frowned.

"I know what you want," he said with a businesslike tone of voice.

"Then show me."

He pulled sheets of paper and a street map out of his inside jacket pocket. He spread the map out on the low table, smoothed it flat. He handed her the sheets of paper that the real estate consultant had sent him. In the upper right hand corner of the sheets of paper with addresses Burnett thought she might be interested in, he'd made a red X with a permanent marking pen. A separate sheet of paper had the name Fitch and a phone number written on it. Angela leaned forward, concentrating, softly biting her lower lip. He watched her.

She went on concentrating for a few minutes, giving particular attention to the pages marked with a red X. The red ink gave them weight, although she knew she'd make her own decision and didn't count on his judgment. But he'd made a good job of what she'd asked him to do. She'd hooked him just like that. Angela lifted her eyes and smiled at him. She let the robe fall open offering him a view, then thought better of it and covered her knees.

Burnett got up and went to the kitchen to refill his glass. When he got back to the living room, Angela was bent over the map. He stood behind her, looking over her shoulder. She made a tracing with her finger along a street on the Southside. The fabric of her robe was completely dry. He looked at her shoulders, the part of her neck that was exposed. He walked around her and sat down in the straight chair. Her eyes went from the map to the sheets of paper spread out on her knees. She took a very deep breath, held it. She wore a faint smile.

"Take your time," Burnett said. His tone was strangely detached. He knew that he wasn't going to get anywhere with her today. "Check them out. I've gone over them with a fine-tooth comb. Now it's up to you."

Angela didn't reply. Not even a look. She exhaled, then reached for her glass and downed the whisky in a gulp. She looked up at Burnett. He gave her a half-smile.

She didn't really see him because she was staring at a point just beyond his head, as though to unfocus her eyes. She saw the blinds drawn in front of the windows. A world existed beyond the firm guard of those blinds, and the map in front of her represented in two dimensions the limitless world she wanted to explore in herself. She put the tip of her index finger in her mouth and rolled her tongue around it.

Her pose was a kind of provocation. Burnett wanted to say something. A throbbing urge blasted at him from the whisky in his stomach and the bare legs and lithe hips of the woman in front of him. He could smell what he couldn't see between her legs. She blushed slightly. He put his drink down, the ice clinked against the glass. She seemed to know what he was thinking and shook her head. It wasn't an invitation.

So Burnett left the apartment frustrated, walking with a slavish posture. He moved slowly along the sidewalk to Birch Street, and then kept on going to Second. The branches of trees reached out above his head and pressed down on him. He grew shorter and shorter until he was only a couple of inches tall. He lit a cigarette, turned around, walked back to Birch. The color of the satin robe came flaring up in his eyes and he winced and bit hard at his lip. The cigarette tasted bitter. He threw it away. That was when he unlocked the car door and got in.

Shimura took off his glasses and set them down on his desk at the Kawamura Agency. His eyes were tired. He gathered the papers in front of him and arranged them in a folder and put the folder in the open file drawer of the cabinet behind him to his left. He swiveled his chair and looked at the clutter on his desk. Shimura scratched absently at his chin. He didn't want the cigarette he was thinking about right now. There wasn't anything to motivate him to straighten up his desk. He was waiting for eight o'clock. There was an hour to kill.

He got up from his desk, left the office, and walked down the hallway past several empty offices until he got to the room that he liked most at the agency, a storage room with a futon and a refrigerator. He heard Kawamura's personal secretary, Asami, at her desk in front of Kawamura's office. Shimura turned the handle of the storage room door and went in. He switched on the overhead light.

It was a small, six-tatami-mat room crowded with filing cabinets and individual heavy-duty cardboard boxes holding alphabetically arranged files and photographs. Metal Venetian blinds covered the two windows. The futon was in a corner of the room. He dragged it out and put it down on the floor in the remaining, empty space, found a linen sheet and threw it over the futon and stretched out on it, lying on his back with his hands clasped behind his head. He stared at the ceiling, then drifted off to sleep.

He woke up a half-hour later grateful to have had some rest. He looked at his watch. It was almost time to go. He put the futon back in the corner and folded the linen sheet. In his office he put his reading glasses on and picked up a spiral-bound notebook. He opened the notebook to the page where he'd written down a car registration number. He copied the number on a separate piece of paper. The car belonged to someone involved in one of Shimura's investigations.

Asami wasn't only Kawamura's personal secretary, she did the research for all the investigators at the Kawamura Agency. She looked up from her desk when Shimura came in wearing his lightweight jacket and a serious expression on his face. She liked Shimura in a friendly way, but she wasn't on anything but working terms with the rest of the investigators at the Kawamura Agency except Kawamura himself, a man on the order of something special because she was in love with him.

Shimura handed her the piece of paper with the registration number on it, grinning with only one side of his mouth. He didn't say anything.

She gave it a once-over, then frowned and gave it back to him. "I can't read it," she said. "Your handwriting's a mess."

"I'll write it again."

He bent over the desk and carefully wrote the number on a sheet of paper lying next to a road atlas and a three-ring binder three inches thick. He stood up straight, drew a long, brave breath. Asami looked down at the registration number.

"Okay," she said. "I'll do what I can."

"As quick as you can," he said. "Please."

Asami tilted her head. "Shimura-*san*, when did I ever hold you back in your work? You've got nothing to worry about. I'll have it for you right away." She let her breath out with what was almost a laugh.

Her words acted on his ears like needles, his eyes narrowed.

"I guess I'm just a little bit on edge," he explained. "Tomiko's on a layover—out of town."

She studied him. "And you look tired."

"I do?"

"Working too much, I suppose?"

"That's right."

"And it's far too late for you to be going home."

"You're right, and I'd like to wring your neck for it, but you work here," he said, smiling at her.

"Just take care of yourself—" and her voice was down close to a whisper.

Shimura nodded his head.

She blushed, then very slowly looked into his eyes. Her face broke into a sunny smile.

⊰ Shimura almost collided with Kawamura, who was busy looking down at his leather-soled shoes that needed polish and not paying attention to where he was walking. They bowed silently and grinned at each other.

"Well, Kawamura-*san*," Shimura said politely.

"I just arrived," Kawamura replied. "I'll take the responsibility."

"Responsibility?"

"For my clumsiness."

Shimura adopted a placating tone. "Kawamura-*san*, I understand how you feel." He was thinking of his exchange with Asami. "I'll be going." He bowed hurriedly and started to walk away.

"Can't you stay?" Kawamura asked without wanting him to say yes.

"No, I have an appointment."

"Well, tomorrow then."

"Tomorrow, Kawamura-*san*." He bowed again, then left Kawamura for the elevator.

⊰ Kawamura swung open the agency door and shut it quickly behind him. He passed Asami and nodded in her direction, went directly to his office and shut the door. He took a small box out of his trousers pocket and opened it, looking at the ring and the stone in it that sparkled with the light of the desk lamp. He snapped the box shut and put it on the desk. Kawamura stared blankly at the stack of unopened mail. He sat in his chair and hauled his legs up, resting the heels of his shoes on the edge of the desk. He shut his eyes, rubbed his forehead with his hand. He heard Aoyama and Eto talking to each other on their way out of the agency.

Kawamura heard the outer door close. No one was left in the agency that could get in the way of what he wanted to do. Small circles of perspiration grew into large patches of moisture under his arms, staining the crisp, pressed shirt. Now, he told himself.

Asami sat at her desk, her slender fingers holding an open file and her thin lips silently shaping the words she read. Kawamura stood a couple of feet away from her, his eyes full of admiration. It was eight o'clock. She should've gone home by now. He took a step forward, leaned against the door frame. Asami turned her head away from the file and looked at him. Kawamura stood up straight, his hands folded behind his back, holding the small box, and his fingers caressed the smooth imitation leather that covered it. He took a faltering step forward. It was almost too much for him.

Kawamura went to the desk. Without saying a word, he gave her the box. He was blushing.

"What is it?"

"For you." Kawamura bowed slightly.

She pushed her chair back away from the desk, turned the box over in her hands. At last she flipped it open with her fingertips. A ring with an amethyst stared back at her. She smiled, then bit her lower lip.

"You love me, don't you?" Kawamura asked politely.

"You know how I feel, Kawamura-*san*."

"It's really true? There's no mistake?"

She lowered her head and fidgeted.

He focused on the black hair of her downcast forehead.

"Yes." Asami looked up at him, her cheeks were bright red.

"Maybe, if you do this, you'll regret it. I'm a lot older than you are."

"No, I never will," she said. "That won't happen."

Kawamura reached out and swiftly took the box from her. He hadn't felt so impatient about reaching a destination for a long time. He put the ring on her finger.

"Now, we're engaged," Asami said, smiling.

Kawamura bent over and kissed her on the mouth. Asami sucked long and hard on his tongue like a vacuum cleaner.

14

Angela tossed the robe on the bed. She wasn't wearing anything underneath it. She slipped on a pair of panties and sat down on the edge of the bed to examine her toes. She rubbed her feet stimulating the blood flow before putting on a pair of thin gray socks. She chose a lightweight short-waisted sweater and pulled it over her head. A pair of loose-fitting lint-white trousers was draped over the back of a chair. She put them on and buttoned them up. She looked at herself in a full-length mirror. She had a small, dangling silver ring in place of the diamond she wore in her navel.

She flicked the ring with her finger, then pulled it down and outward. She sat on the edge of the bed again and brushed her hair. She pinched her cheeks, got up and went to the mirror and put on lipstick. She put her feet into a pair of high tops and loosely tied the laces. On her way out she picked up the map and sheets of paper Burnett had brought with him.

¶ The streets were busy with people and traffic. She hailed a taxi at the corner of Edgewater and Prospect. They drove off in a direction away from the lake. She got out of the taxi in midtown, walked two blocks, turned the corner, and hailed another taxi on State Street. She tilted her head back and stared at the roof of the taxi. There were several scratches that might've been from a pair of high heels. She smiled, playing with the ring in her navel. They were heading northwest toward the river and a neighborhood with its industrial buildings converted to condominiums and lofts.

Angela leaned out the open window and took a breath of polluted air. The night sky hung low over the city. The air was humid and cool and a soft wind moved the pollution around without getting rid of it. When they got to Pleasant Street they crossed the river and

turned right onto Third Street going north. It wasn't the right place.
There were a lot of people walking down the sidewalks, some of them
carried groceries, paper bags with bottles in them, flowers wrapped
in newspaper, plastic containers of takeout meals.

She told the driver to continue north and they went on until the
neighborhood changed to a part of the city she didn't know. The taxi
slowed down, edging forward in traffic past the flashing neon of a
couple of bars and a striptease club with a big, greasy-looking man
at the door. The faces of passersby were green, red, yellow and blue.
The taxi jerked forward and Angela sat back in the seat, shut her eyes
a minute, and when she opened them the driver was still on Third
heading toward Beverly Avenue, but he turned short of it on Orchard
Street. They slowed down in front of the address she'd given him
and she knew right away that she didn't like it. She told the driver to
move on, traffic thinned out, and they were driving through dimly
lighted streets.

Man-made colors jumped out of currents of electricity again as
the taxi made a turn onto Harding Street into the glare of a half-dozen
neon signs. The driver asked her if he could stop for cigarettes and
because she'd hired him for at least a couple of hours it didn't matter
to her if he bought a pack of cigarettes or called his wife or girlfriend
to say he'd be coming home late or if he'd wanted a glass of beer. He
pulled over to the curb in front of an all-night grocery. A bus made
its way clumsily around the taxi.

The driver lit a cigarette and they pulled away from the curb,
heading south. It took them more than twenty minutes to get to the
Southside, and the taxi turned on Euclid Avenue, at the nineteenth-
century church, continued along Euclid until it turned left on Sunset
Avenue and right on West Mineral Street, then slowed down in the
middle of it surrounded by wood frame houses with wooden porches
anchored by stone pillars, and descending stone stairs to flats below
street level. Angela rolled down the window to get a better look at
the houses on the street. Here and there the sidewalk was buckled by
the shallow spreading roots of an oak tree. A couple walked their dog
down the sidewalk beneath the glow of streetlights.

Angela shook her head, she wasn't interested in this address either, and the driver continued on West Mineral, turned left at Booth Street, left on Drake Avenue, left on Sunset and back to Euclid. The sky was painted with stars that weren't lost in the overall glow of the city's lights, and they blinked knowingly at her as she stared up at them through the open window. The taxi was going to Pigsville.

When they got there she asked the driver to stop on a deserted street. Cars hummed and rumbled past them. The taxi engine idled, and she looked out at the sort of neighborhood she'd been looking for all night. She gave the driver an address taken from her sheets of paper. They turned right at the next block and came to a halt in front of one of the many one-story four-room wooden houses lined up on each side of Nightingale Lane. This was it. She thought for an instant about what she'd done in order to get to this address in Pigsville. She had played the game with the vibrator, and then fucked Burnett so he'd do what she asked him to do, and she'd liked it up to a point, and that's what had got her here. Angela's eyes were fixed on a yellow-ish light shining dully through a window shade.

⊰ Angela gave the taxi driver an address not far from her own, around the corner on Second and Lafayette, because she didn't want him leaving her at an address he'd write down in a logbook that could later be traced to her. She got out at the corner beneath a streetlight, paid the driver what she owed him and gave him a generous tip and put his business card in her wallet. There might be a next time and she liked the way he knew the city.

Alone in the apartment, she undressed and put on her satin robe and tied the belt around her narrow waist before setting the water to boil for instant noodle soup.

15

Pohl finished his first drink less than a minute after the bartender set it down. He got to the Casino Club a good half-hour before the time he'd arranged to meet Shimura, and he was sure that his friend knew it because he'd been doing the same thing, arriving early for every appointment for pleasure or business, since they were in high school together.

He repeatedly picked up and put down the empty glass, made intersecting rings on the bar counter, and stared at the gold letters that spelled out the name Casino Club on the rim of the smoky glass ashtray with a burning cigarette and two extinguished butts of the same brand. He swiveled on the bar stool to get a better look at the club. The booths and tables were packed with customers. He was satisfied that he didn't know anyone in the club tonight. He called the bartender over and ordered another drink, then finished his cigarette, happily flicking ashes in the ashtray.

Pohl was thirsty and hungry. He asked the bartender for a glass of water and a snack to tide him over until dinner. The bartender returned with a pitcher of ice water and a bowl of fresh fish eyes in some sort of spicy sauce. Pohl popped one in his mouth and chewed it slowly, savoring it. Juice dribbled down his chin. He dabbed at the juice with a paper napkin. Pouring himself a glass of ice water, he drank it down in one gulp.

Shimura arrived on time. He went straight to the bar. There was a lot of noise in the restaurant adjacent to the bar. Shimura's eyes went from table to table, booth to booth, looking at the faces of the customers. A young woman licking an ice cream bar caught his eye. He smiled at her pixie-ish face. He sat down next to Pohl, folded his hands on the bar, ordered an aniseed vodka on the rocks. Then he looked at the bowl of fish eyes.

"How can you eat that?" Shimura's face twisted with disgust.

"I like them."

Pohl picked up a couple of moist fish eyes and rolled them around between his fingers before dropping them into his mouth. He chewed and swallowed, wiping away the spicy juice and smacking his lips. Another glass of water, then he ran his tongue across his upper front teeth.

"All right, you don't have to make a show of it," Shimura said, taking a sip from his glass.

"They're better in pairs," Pohl confided.

"I'm sure they are."

Pohl pushed the bowl of fish eyes away, looking intently at Shimura. His face was drawn into a frown. "I want to forget about it. Maybe if I forget about it, it'll just be wind or dust."

"Poetic. Angela?" Shimura asked.

"Angela." Pohl finished his whisky, put the glass down and picked it up and put it down, making more intersecting rings on the bar. He was far away.

"What is it?"

Without answering, Pohl smiled bitterly, waved at the bartender and ordered another drink. Shimura nursed his. Pohl looked at Shimura and said: "I wish I could forget it. It doesn't do me any good to remember."

"Remember what? Will you please tell me what's going on."

Shimura was losing his patience. His feet were hot and the heat rose slowly to his head. It was a ball of heat like a peach pit and when it rose it scratched the lining of his stomach and throat and nose. He pinched his nose shut to keep the peach pit from coming out.

"I haven't slept a wink," Pohl said. His body jerked slightly.

"You've been awake all this time?"

"I'm the one to blame. It's not what you think."

"I'm not thinking anything."

"No uninvited guests! That's my motto from now on. And don't go poking your nose into what's none of your business."

"Two mottos."

"That's right." Pohl sipped from his glass of whisky. "Maybe if

I'd pay less attention to her she'd pay more attention to me. That's the way it works with women."

Pohl laughed at his own words.

A strangely perverse laugh, it chilled his friend, who picked up his aniseed vodka, drank it down, and waved at the bartender for another.

"Let's have it," Shimura said, looking at Pohl's steady hands. "What's worrying you?"

Pohl took a deep breath and exhaled slowly. He pushed aside the glass of whisky, tired of it and almost everything else, and plucked two fish eyes from the bowl, chewing and swallowing methodically. Not a drop of juice spilled down his chin. He combed his hair back with his hand, smiled at Shimura, who returned a sincere smile of his own, then told him the story of what he'd seen when he'd crept into Angela's apartment.

"She wasn't alone," Pohl concluded, pinching two fish eyes between his fingers, then putting them in his mouth. "There was someone there with her, and I didn't see his face."

Shimura switched his gaze from Pohl's sad eyes to the ceiling. Pohl took his hand away from his cheek, his longish hair fell in front of his eyes and he stared through the strands at Shimura. Shimura looked warmly at Pohl. Pohl averted his eyes, cleared his throat, shrugged.

"What do you make of it?" Pohl asked, his voice almost a whisper. "I saw what I wasn't supposed to see, okay. I want to know the truth. I want to know his name. Then I'd like to forget the whole thing."

"There are things you've got to forget at any cost," Shimura said.

"If that's true, fine," Pohl said. "Any cost."

Shimura heaved a long sigh.

"What about making an investigation?" Pohl asked. "Will you do it? No matter what's going on between them I won't interfere. I won't interfere or meddle with them or cause you any trouble. I want to know who he is and if she loves him. Then I'll know if I've got a chance."

"You're my friend. I'll do it," Shimura said without hesitating.

Pohl plunged his fingers into the bowl and came up with three fish eyes, shook them like dice in a loose fist, then popped them in his mouth.

"If you go on eating those things you *must* be hungry."

"That's right," Pohl said, smiling. "Let's get out of here."

The bartender handed Pohl a special towel, moist and hot, scented with lemon, to wash the smell of the spicy fish eyes off his hands. Shimura went ahead to the exit of the Casino Club. Pohl paid the bill.

⁋ Jackson Street was crowded with people sniffing the fresh night air under the glow of neon lights. Pohl and Shimura went in the direction of their favorite Italian restaurant. On the way, a dog walked toward them with one eye shut and a sticky secretion in the other. The fur covering his ribcage was dyed blue. Pohl turned his head and his eyes filled with blue neon from an arcade with coin-operated games. Shimura patted the dog on the head as it went by. The dog snapped at him, growling.

At the traffic signal, Pohl saw a roving beam of light behind him and followed it up to a woman standing on a small balcony with a standard flashlight in her hand. She directed a trembling circle of light over the sidewalk that must have been impossible to see from where she stood like a watchtower guard looking for an escaped prisoner.

Trying hard to focus on the woman, who remained a silhouette in the faint light behind her, Pohl narrowed his eyes, and for all he could see she was alone, the silhouette of a solitary woman, standing straight as a soldier looking for something she'd never find. She tapped her foot impatiently on the balcony, switched off the flashlight. Shimura tugged Pohl's sleeve, pulling him across the intersection, and he looked back from the middle of the crosswalk at the empty balcony. Pohl followed Shimura to the other side of the street. The restaurant was in the middle of the block.

The County Sheriff's Office, founded in 1835, is the largest and oldest sheriff's office in the state. The constitutional mandates include keeping and maintaining the peace throughout the county, maintaining the county jail, providing bailiff services for circuit courts and serving legal process. It is comprised of four Bureaus: Administration, Police Services, Special Operations, and Detention Services.

When Captain Rand Hadley retired from the County Sheriff's Office under the "Rule of 75" (when an officer's age, added to years of service, equaled the number 75), he'd been working in the CID (Criminal Investigation Division) for several years. He served a total of twenty-seven years in a variety of assignments throughout the department including Process, Patrol, Parks, Transit, Courts, Detention Bureau, Airport, Police Services Bureau — HIDTA (High Intensity Drug Trafficking Areas), and the Drug Enforcement Unit. He had a Bachelor of Science-Criminal Justice degree from the local branch of the state university, and was a graduate of the Department of Justice's Death Investigation School and the Midwestern University School of Police Staff and Command.

Randall Hadley was sitting in the small kitchen wearing a plaid bathrobe and scraping the burnt patches off his breakfast toast when the doorbell rang. It was eight-thirty. Morning sunlight came in through the window and warmed the Formica tabletop. Steam drifted up from his mug of freshly brewed coffee. He took a sip of it before he got up to answer the door.

When he opened it, Shimura stood in front of him in a beige jacket, navy shirt and beige trousers, and a cigar between his lips.

"You can't smoke that in here," Hadley said, pulling the door all the way open.

"You don't have to tell me, Rand. Give me an ashtray."

Hadley turned around, headed for the kitchen, and Shimura followed him. He looked at the familiar, sparsely furnished one-bedroom apartment where he'd visited Hadley so many times in the last ten years.

Rand Hadley gave him personal or professional advice when he couldn't find a solution to a problem on his own. He'd spent the better part of the night out with Pohl after dinner in the Italian restaurant, and he had a hangover and didn't know how to handle the thing Pohl wanted him to do. The personal favor to Pohl would have to be something independent of the Kawamura Agency and it required tact.

Shimura sat down at the kitchen table opposite Hadley. There was a large empty ashtray in front of him and he put his cigar in it. Hadley picked up a slice of toast he'd spread with cholesterol-reducing butter substitute. He'd quit smoking a year ago, had high cholesterol, and he wasn't in great shape because he liked to eat although he didn't cook for himself, so he'd begun to pay attention to what he put in his stomach. The burnt toast made a lot of noise as he chewed it.

He was fifty-four years old, divorced, and he taught investigative basics in the community and technical colleges system, which gave him a meager salary that filled the gap left by his county pension equal to 2.5 percent earned, per year of service, of the average of his high three consecutive years of earnings. The maximum pension a detective drew was eighty percent.

"How are you feeling?"

"Do you know what happens to someone hit by a slow freight?"

"Cut the kidding, Rand. You haven't looked better in months."

"Everything I like to eat I can't have and everything I can have isn't what I'd pick if I had the choice, so how do you expect me to look at it? It's boring, but you're right. I'm feeling better, looking better."

Rand Hadley cracked a smile, took a swallow of coffee.

"I'm sorry, I forgot to offer you a cup."

He got up, took a mug out of the cabinet and poured Shimura a cup of steaming coffee. He gave him the mug and sat down again.

"You're looking tired," Hadley said. "You work too hard."

"That's funny, coming from you."

"Did I tell you I got a letter from my ex-wife?"

"No, what did she want?"

"More money. But she's right. I owe her."

"Did she say that?"

"No, she wouldn't say a thing like that. We get along just fine."

"And you take care of her and your kid just fine, Rand."

"We've been divorced two years, and in the years we had together before that, after I retired, I still wasn't able to make it up to her."

"It's the same old song, isn't it? Whether you're private or public."

"A detective? Well, facts are facts. Policemen's wives have it tough."

"What's she going to do with more money that she can't do with the money she's got now? She has a job."

"The kid's going to college, and it costs plenty because it isn't a community college, and he's not bright enough to have a scholarship —I've got to call a spade a spade—and I don't want him taking a loan. You never get out from under a loan."

"True."

"Anyway, I wasn't spending much before, and now that I won't be eating in restaurants—or smoking cigarettes, even—I'll have to learn to cook for myself, and then I'll have money to spare."

Hadley finished his cup of coffee, got up, went to the sink and rinsed it. He put it in the drying rack, and without turning around, he asked: "What is it?"

"What?"

"I'm always happy to see you, you know that, but what's on your mind?"

"Burt Pohl."

"Burt?"

"And the agency."

"You had any breakfast?"

"Not yet."

"Let me fix you some bacon and eggs—you can tell me about it."

Rand Hadley didn't wait for an answer, he took a frying pan down from a hook on the wall, switched on the gas burner, went to the refrigerator for eggs, bacon and a cholesterol-reducing butter substitute for cooking.

Burnett undressed slowly, his arms and legs weighed more than his whole body and he could barely stand up. He put his hand to his forehead. He didn't have a fever. Wearing only his underpants, he went to the study and stood at the window next to his desk and separated the Venetian blinds to look down at the street. There was the car with blackened windows that had followed him since he'd gone out to check the locations the real estate agent had given him. He placed his hands on the sill and peered through the blinds at the car and sighed. He wondered now what his sexual adventures had got him into.

He looked down at the erection that pushed against his boxer shorts, pointing northeast. His right hand was more than averagely dexterous, he kept his left on the sill, and he touched himself beneath the crisply laundered fabric. His cock jumped, his fingers were cold. No circulation, he thought. He went on looking at the car. The headlights blinked on and off like a pair of eyes. His right hand came out of his boxer shorts, he jumped back, away from the window. It was the wrong time for pleasure even though that's what he looked for all the time. He suddenly felt sick, ran to the toilet and vomited.

⸾ Burnett took off his boxer shorts, turned the shower on and got in, letting the warm water flow over him. In three-minute cycles he experienced severe muscular stomach cramps accompanied by spasms until he regulated the temperature to a higher degree of heat. This calmed him down. The telephone rang but he didn't leave the comfort of the shower to answer it because he was sure it was Violet Archer, who had the worst timing of any woman he'd known.

Violet called from the public phone at the corner whenever she saw the light of the desk lamp shining through the blinds like a signal he'd given her. He loved Violet's slanted green eyes, and after he'd finished with her, though it'd taken him a long time to get some distance between them and still she clung to him like lint, he thought of her eyes blinking and tearful with the pain he'd happily inflicted on her lithesome body. The phone rang, Burnett went on scrubbing himself under the shower, and he let it ring until she hung up.

Violet left the Kawamura Agency with a worried look on her face. Even Kawamura noticed it when she went past the open door of his office. Shimura hadn't turned up anything for her on Burnett. There was nothing she could use against him. She wanted to squeeze money out of him, and she'd hired Shimura to give her something to hold on to. Violet figured that Burnett owed her more than money, but it was money that she was most likely to get out of him, and losing money hurt him more than anything else. Violet went straight to the elevator, fixing her hair in front of the mirror while she waited.

She stood on the sidewalk in front of the building where the agency occupied the sixth floor. The soft wind blew her jet-black hair across her face. She caught a few strands with her fingertips and put them in her mouth. Her green eyes, slanted like wings, looked down at her feet. With plenty of money, she would've been accepted by the world. It was money that made happiness, and her own happiness was the only thing she thought about. Now she was hungry.

∦ The restaurant on Waterford Street near the river was small. There were a dozen tables and they were all occupied. A middle-aged woman folded her napkin, set it down next to an empty soup bowl and a torn piece of French bread and got up from her chair. Violet waited for her to leave the table, and the waitress cleared it and laid out place-mat, napkin and cutlery.

The waitress waved Violet to the table and was handed the lamin-ated menu. She was hungry, but she watched her weight. She ordered a green salad and an omelet. She sipped absentmindedly from the glass of water. She knew that she looked good, and it was obvious that a lot of men were attracted to her. She'd got mixed up with Bur-nett because she'd wanted it with him, and he was always looking for women. But why did she have to find men like Burnett, who only abused her?

She didn't know until she was involved with him that he had a particular way with women and what he wanted them to do for him, even expected of them right up to the moment he was finished with them. She ate her omelet slowly, chewing each mouthful twenty times before swallowing, drinking room-temperature bottled water, and kept the salad for last. Most of the customers left the restaurant to return to work.

Violet put her hand between her legs and pushed the hem of her skirt high enough to touch a raised part of the skin on her inner thigh. It was a scar Burnett gave her during one of his games. She'd agreed to it, but it left her with a permanent, discolored ridge on the silkiness near her pussy. She pulled down the hem of her skirt, shifting her legs under the table.

She put her hand to her mouth. She touched her full lips with the fingers that had caressed the blemish. It was the only imperfection on her skin. She vowed to get even with Burnett. She bit gently on her lower lip, pouting.

Her hands itched, she reached for the glass of water just to do something with one of them, wanting the uncomfortable feeling to go away, and when it didn't go away she thought a slap in the face might do the trick. Instead, she quickly swallowed a mouthful of water, a few drops ran down her chin. She ignored them. She took a deep breath, then finished the salad, spearing slices of tomato with her fork. Violet ordered coffee. When she finished it the waitress re-filled the cup.

⫟ She left the restaurant and wasn't in a hurry to go anywhere though she knew what she was going to do at nightfall. It was late afternoon now, people walked slowly along the sidewalk window-shopping. She watched them as if they couldn't see her. She gave the younger, wealthy-looking men a perfect examination with her eyes. It made them uncomfortable. They gazed back at her, taking stock of every line and curve, trying not to draw attention to themselves. Some of them stared thoroughly, boldly at Violet Archer, their eyes sharp as razors climbing slowly from her shoes to her black hair.

Burnett hadn't looked at her like that, but he was smart. The transparent ones didn't appeal to Violet Archer. Burnett didn't let it happen right away, he kept his interest in her just beneath the surface out of sight. He played the hand he held just to get her, and he didn't use the same cards again.

Violet saw him once or twice a week if he wanted it that way whether or not she was in the mood to see him. He never told her she was anything more than someone to play with and that was what kept her from leaving him. She liked it. And she liked the games he played with her even when they hurt. Then he was bored, it was over, he dumped her, and it threw her out of balance. Now she'd get something out of him that would make her happy. He was going to pay for his indifference and the scar between her legs.

¶ She went to a department store open late Thursday nights. On the ground floor, she bought cosmetics and paid more than she was used to spending on them. She took the escalator to the fourth floor, bought a set of underwear, panties and bra, and then looked at clothes. She didn't want to buy anything, but she tried on a short, beryl-blue dress that complemented her slanted green eyes. The salesgirl stood next to her as she looked in the mirror and told her she was just like a television star. Violet left the dress in the changing room. She wasn't interested in television. Her eyes looked good enough without a beryl-blue dress.

It was after seven and the department store closed at eight. Violet went through the swinging doors and onto the sidewalk and hailed a taxi. She gave the driver her address, left her purchases just inside the door of her apartment, then went downstairs and got back into the taxi and gave the driver an address a block away from where Burnett lived.

Frankie Lundquist, a driver who did freelance surveillance work for the Kawamura Agency, was behind the wheel of the car with blackened windows, following two car lengths behind Burnett who was cruising along the Midwestern city streets heading home. His car made a turn and he drove into the garage and she pulled up to the curb and parked in the failing twilight near his apartment building. It was the second day she'd been following him.

Shimura had asked for her because she was the best driver they had outside the agency. The two in-house drivers were busy today. She was called to Shimura's office where she picked up the keys and was told what she had to know about Burnett from what he'd learned from his client, Violet Archer. He gave her the description and registration number of the car. He handed her a camera with a telephoto lens and an agency notebook. He wrote Burnett's address on an advertisement for a sporting shoe he'd torn out of a magazine. He pulled a snapshot of Burnett out of an envelope and gave it to her, waving goodbye, smiling politely.

Shimura didn't know why Violet wanted to know more than she already knew about Burnett. It was an ordinary investigation and whatever else there was to know didn't matter because he was being paid to do a particular job and when he was being paid to do a job he didn't have to think about anything else.

The morning of the third day, Frankie went down the elevator to the garage and checked the gas gauge to see if there was enough in the tank for another day driving around the city following Burnett. She drove the car up the ramp and took it out onto the street. The morning traffic was heavy with cars and buses taking people to work. Frankie went straight to Burnett's apartment building.

She waited for him to come out. He wasn't awake yet, the blinds were drawn. She watched them discreetly with a pair of binoculars. Frankie made a few entries in a notebook that belonged to the agency, jotting down the exact time that she was parked a half-block from the subject's address beneath the overreaching branches of an elm in the early morning sunlight.

The sensation of waiting struck her face like a wet paper towel. It felt good. The sunlight warmed the inside of the car even though the windows were tinted. She put a piece of nicotine chewing gum in her mouth. Burnett came out of the building in a hurry, looked up and down the street, then went back into the building. He came out of the garage in his car and swung left past Frankie. She turned the engine over and followed him.

Her shoes fell forward in the space in front of the passenger seat. She drove barefoot. Her toenails were painted blue, the same color as her eyes. Her teeth were unnaturally white. The polluted sky was without a cloud.

She moved quickly through the awakened city, Burnett was driving ahead of her fast through traffic. Frankie kept a car between them. Burnett rarely changed lanes. Traffic flowed smoothly until he turned right at Normandy and they came up on a jam with a truck stopped in the middle of Normandy and a man unloading a couple of wooden crates, using a hand truck to cart them through the entrance of a glass and steel building. Frankie ran her tongue across her front teeth, stuck her head out the side window, looked back, and saw the cars lined up behind her.

Two more crates were unloaded and placed on the hand truck and pushed into the building. A car sounded its horn. She saw the back of Burnett's head, two cars up, through the windshield of the car in front of her. She looked down at her bare feet. The thick air that filled the street was amber-colored. Her eyes wandered past her toes to the clutch pedal, brake and accelerator over to the other side and her shoes. She liked the color of her shoes. She took the nicotine gum from her mouth and threw it out the window. A glint of sunlight caught her eyes. She winced.

She heard a grating sound and turned her head. A trash can standing in an alcove inched forward, scraped against the cement under it. A bare, brown leg came out from behind the trash can and the foot at the end of the leg wore an orange sneaker and the sneaker swung from side to side on its heel. She stared at it.

The trash can went on scraping the cement and it seemed to scrape at the inside of her head as it was pushed further out of the alcove to give more room to whoever was sitting behind it. An arm waved wildly around one of the handles, fingers gripped it, and the hand pushed the trash can far enough to the right for Frankie to see the eyes of a pimply-faced teenager wearing a Hawaiian shirt and peacock-blue shorts. Frankie winked at him, giving him a glimpse of her white teeth, but he didn't see her. The trash can continued its scraping as the boy got to his feet, looking disoriented. He struck the side of trash can with a jerk of his knee and the lid fell off, making a clanging noise. He ran off and she watched him fade in the rearview mirror.

The truck was finished unloading, started up and went on along Normandy, turned right at Midland Road. Burnett followed the car behind the truck but didn't turn at Midland, just headed west on Normandy until he got to Glendale Avenue going north to the city limits.

Frankie tailed him into various neighborhoods each with a different look and a different population, and there was nothing about them that gave her the slightest idea of what he was doing in them. She didn't know what he was up to, but it wasn't her job to find out anything more than the details of what he did for the length of time she was following him. She shook her head. It wasn't going to be easy for anyone to make anything stick together from her report.

She'd almost filled her notebook with the names of streets and districts Burnett passed through and where he stopped his car and got out, and in the margins she indicated the time of each significant pause in his onward course with a description of what he did, when he got out of the car. She photographed him. She watched him through the telephoto lens of the camera that belonged to the Kawamura Agency.

Burnett did pretty much the same thing each time he pulled over to the curb just like he had a ritual to follow, without thought or improvisation. No jerky movements, but smooth, synchronized gestures. He switched off the engine and got out of the car and stretched his legs. He spread a city map out on the roof of the car, pressing his thumbnail into the crease to flatten it. He stared at what was in front of him. He held several loose sheets of paper, going through them with wide-open eyes. The sheets were fanned like playing cards in his hand. He checked the map against what was written on the sheets of paper, standing on tiptoe, leaning forward, with his weight on the door frame.

In the next moment he produced a red marking pen, raised it to shoulder height and made a stabbing gesture with it to mark the map. Looking satisfied, Burnett folded the map and put the map and papers on the front seat and got in after them, started the car and drove away.

She had no clear sense of the passing time. It could have been a moment or two, it could have been hours. She checked the gas gauge. She was chewing her fifth piece of nicotine gum when Burnett turned the corner and went down the ramp to the garage under his building. She parked a half-block away, shut off the engine, threw the gum out the window.

Frankie closed her eyes and pressed on her lids with her fingertips. She opened her eyes. It was the last instant of twilight before nightfall and the beauty of it gave her the idea taking in a lungful of air. The air was like sweet syrup going into her mouth and nostrils. She tapped her fingers on the steering wheel. She saw a light and Burnett's silhouette behind the Venetian blinds in his study. She noted in the log the time that she witnessed the subject was at home.

She looked up from it and saw a pedestrian running down the middle of the street after a dog, and they were shadows running in a direction away from her in the night, shadows that looked like they weren't really there. An oncoming car didn't see them. It bore down on them and was going to knock them down. A woman ran out of a phone booth and into the street waving her arms and shouting at them. Frankie flashed her headlights at the oncoming car and its headlights switched to high beams and the car swerved around the man and the dog.

The bright headlights burned through her lids, and she kept her eyes shut until the car had gone past. She opened her eyes, checked her watch against the clock in the dashboard, opened the agency notebook and ran her finger down the lines indicating the alternating time schedule. Eto was on his way to replace her. She was going to knock off and go straight home the minute he got there.

20

Pohl sighed into the telephone, then said goodnight. Shimura listened to the click of the receiver, an emptiness, then hung up. Pohl had wanted to hear something but he didn't have anything new to tell him because he hadn't had much time to spend checking on the man that Pohl had seen in Angela's apartment. Shimura glanced at the clock on the wall. It was eleven-twenty.

He went to the kitchen to have something to eat. He couldn't decide what he wanted, it was late, and there weren't lot of things to choose from in the refrigerator. There was leftover pheasant, eggs, tortillas, yogurt, strawberries. A recipe came to his mind.

> *Stir-fry pheasant breasts*
> *in extra virgin olive oil*
> *with two crushed cloves of garlic.*
> *Blend in tomato paste while frying.*
> *Toast tortillas lightly.*

While he was thinking about the pheasant tortillas something jumped up in his memory, got in the way of his appetite, made a sideways movement, hopping up and down, then faded out to make room again for the hunger in his stomach. He stared at the contents of the refrigerator, then looked in one of the kitchen cabinets. He didn't have all the ingredients for fresh salsa. He peeled the aluminum foil from the leftover pheasant, smelled the cooked flesh, smiled. He lit the stove. A nearly perfect quarter moon shone through the kitchen window.

Shimura finished the pheasant tortillas, wiped his mouth with a napkin, then fixed a cup of instant coffee, black. He sat at the kitchen table, manipulating a toothpick in the spaces between his teeth. He looked down at the empty plate without moving more than the fingers using the toothpick to find and dislodge particles of pheasant and corn tortilla. What was left of the pheasant tortillas stared back at him.

Then he saw the picture of Burnett as if it were in front of him, the one he'd given to Frankie, and he compared it with the poorly sketched counterpart Pohl had given him in the Casino Club, a portrait of the man he'd seen at Angela's apartment. Something clicked in his head, it wasn't a big noise but he heard it clearly. It didn't hurt and it didn't seem real but it made one whole thing out of two separate things and that one thing forced him out of his chair at the same time as he stabbed his gums with the toothpick.

Until now it was a crackpot idea. It wasn't even a complete idea now, but it was more than it had been a few minutes ago. He sat down and finished his cup of coffee. The realization swelled like a massive wave and it crashed against him and he rubbed his chin with his hand and grinned.

21

Violet got out of the taxi. She wasn't far from Burnett's apartment. She walked slowly along the sidewalk on East Olive Street, almost daydreaming, and went past the entrance of Burnett's building to the corner, crossed the street and turned around and went back the way she'd come until she stopped at the public phone. She stood in front of it without opening the doors. The sky was dark and the street was busy with a steady flow of traffic in both directions. Now and then someone hurried along the sidewalk.

Violet looked up, and her anger at Burnett made the sky look like an endless field of dark ice. There was nothing left in it of the sunset. Just stars that looked like sparkling chips of ice or pinpoints of light embedded in an ice block. The darkness in the expression on her face went up into the sky and bounced back down straight into her heart.

She swung the phone booth doors open and let them shut behind her, leaning against the glass with her shoulder. She raised her head a little and saw the glow of lamplight behind the Venetian blinds. Burnett was there, and she was going to talk to him.

She dropped some change into the phone, started to press the numbers, then she saw a man running down the middle of the street chasing a dog. A car was coming at them, and she saw that if it went on the way it was going the driver wouldn't see the man or the dog in the faded light and there was going to be a terrible accident. She put the receiver back on the hook, the change tumbled down into the receptacle, ringing in her ears.

She ran out of the phone booth and into the street and waved her arms and shouted at the man chasing the dog to warn him against the danger of the car. She was about to shut her eyes when something made her open them wide instead.

A woman behind the wheel of a car parked a few feet away from the phone booth under the outstretched branches of an elm tree must have seen the potential disaster because all at once the headlights flashed on and went straight into the eyes of the driver bearing down on the man and dog, and the driver switched the headlights to high beams, and together the warning from one and illumination of the other made the driver swerve out of the way at the last instant, and the man and dog were safe and sound in the last breath of twilight. Violet's arms fell to her sides.

Breathing hard, she went back to the phone booth, lifted the receiver, scooped the coins out and dropped them back into the phone and pushed Burnett's number. She waited for him to answer. The telephone rang a dozen times.

She didn't really want to talk to him, she wanted to let off steam. She wanted to tell him to fuck himself. "You might as well bury your money somewhere even a dog couldn't find it because I'm going to take every last cent you've got and leave you with nothing which is what you deserve." The phone went on ringing, no one answered. She didn't say a word. Violet hung up and went home.

22

Shimura looked at the empty coffee cup, dropped the toothpick in it, then smiled at the remains of his meal of pheasant tortillas. He got up from the table and went to the phone on the wall next to the sink, picked up the receiver and dialed Rand Hadley's number. Burnett's face kept jumping into the blank spot that was the face of the man Pohl had seen at Angela's apartment. If he didn't get it off his chest it was going to drive him nuts.

Hadley picked up the phone. "Who is it?" He was wide awake.

"It's late, I know, but I've just had a crazy idea," Shimura said.

"What have you got?"

"I've got Violet Archer and Lew Burnett. And the unidentified man Pohl wants to know more about."

"Okay."

"Now I'm convinced there's some connection between Burnett and Pohl's man, and I can't say why I know it, but my instinct is telling me there's something there and that I've got to follow it up. I always follow my instinct—you taught me that a man's natural intuitive power doesn't lie."

"Don't say another word. I'm sold already. What we're always asking ourselves—if what we feel in our guts is true—is an up-in-the-air question we're waiting to catch. Some people buy it, others don't. You've got to get something solid to go on. You'll need more than a hunch to bring it into focus, you'll need proof. You've got to put Burnett together with Angela."

"Thanks, Rand. I just had to say it out loud."

"Now look, Shimura—"

"I am looking," he said. "I'm looking forward to helping Pohl get a shot at being with Angela. He's waited a long time, Rand, and now it's coming."

"You sure that's what he really wants?"

"That's what he wants, right or wrong."

"Okay, then that's what you've got to do. Goodnight."

Shimura hung up, sighed, switched off the kitchen light, went to the bedroom, got undressed and climbed into bed with a newspaper.

23

Pohl stared at the orchid plant standing as a centerpiece on a dull table strewn with books. Plants were a responsibility, they required the sort of attention he'd rather give an animal or human being, but it was a gift from Angela and it was her way of reaching across a void and making contact with him after what he'd seen going on in her apartment, so he accepted it gladly, and he thought that maybe it was training for something else, a child, because that was what he'd always wanted with her, but he didn't know where she was or what was going on, so he couldn't let himself think about it.

He was sorry that Shimura didn't have anything new to tell him about the man he'd seen in Angela's living room. He didn't have the courage to talk to her himself, he couldn't go that far with something that made him feel so vulnerable, and if he'd had the courage it wouldn't do him any good because she didn't answer the phone when he called.

He was in love with her. He dialed her again. He'd always love her whether she loved him or not. It was after eleven. He listened to the telephone ringing, waited for her to answer without believing she'd pick it up, there was no answer, and he felt his stomach twist into a knot. It went on ringing, he put the receiver down. He paced up and down the living room. He looked at the orchid plant. He wanted to throw it out the window or feed it gasoline or trim it with an axe. He told himself he should've counted the number of times the phone rang, maybe it was an odd number and if it'd turned out to be an odd number it would've been lucky for him. He felt like he had run out of luck.

To change his luck, he wanted to cure himself, get this worrying and sickening thing finished with before it went any further, because if it went further he'd have much difficulty curing it and maybe he wouldn't be able to cure it at all and end up losing everything, including his mind. No matter which way it went, a cure would put a different turn on his luck. He decided to get beat up, to get hurt for how he was letting Angela ruin his life, making him think about her all the time, and maybe that would shake him up enough to let go of what he didn't have a grasp on anyway. He wasn't brave enough to do it by himself. He'd have to go outside and find someone to pick a fight with. That would be the right cure, just what the doctor ordered, and he didn't need an office visit or a prescription, just step outside, sucker, and pick a fight.

It was a good idea because it was a feeling idea and not a thinking idea. He didn't take a jacket, he went out just the way he was dressed. He started walking down Fourteenth Street.

He wasn't going to look for a fight in a bar. A fight with a drunk didn't guarantee that he wouldn't be seriously hurt, and getting himself knocked unconscious wasn't the point. Just a bit of roughing up to loosen the fixed ideas in his head. And anyway a choice like that didn't attract him as much as the thought of something spontaneous right here on the street. He turned onto Jackson at midnight.

Pohl was thinking clearly about this and nothing else, which was proof that the cure had already started working. It was Friday, and he didn't have to work until Monday. He could take a beating tonight and have the weekend to recover from it. He stared straight ahead and kept walking. His mouth watered because he could almost taste the cure, and he wanted it.

He leaned into the first man that brushed past him close enough to make it look like it was not on purpose, just to try it out. He wasn't afraid of what was going to happen to him, but he *was* afraid of what was happening to him because of Angela.

Pohl tried it again with a man who was twice his size. It was almost a head-on collision. He looked up at him, and the man's face had a broad mouth that told him to apologize and the thick lips didn't move and the weight of the demand was in his eyes. Pohl didn't intend to offer one, but he opened his mouth just the same and nothing came out of it. The big man smiled, with a good natured look in his eyes. Pohl wasn't expecting that.

Now there was definitely something wrong with the expression on Pohl's face. He looked more like a crazy dog than a man. The big man, who was almost fat, took a step backward. His mouth was stiff and tight but the corners went up just a little. It wasn't really a smile now, but a calculating look filled with uncertainty. He was trying to figure the odds. It didn't last long, but a smile from Pohl that wasn't really a smile went floating across the sidewalk to the man, and made him shrink into himself.

Pohl took a few steps backward, away from the target, and lowered his head like a goat. He ran straight at the man's belly and butted him, then bounced backward off the protruding stomach, straining his own neck. The stomach was not fat, it was packed solid. The big man looked uncomprehendingly at him. Pohl was busy rubbing the back of his neck, he wasn't paying attention to anything while he was doing it. The fist of the man crashed into the side of his head and sent him staggering sideways. It hit him again, he was he seeing colored sparks from an uppercut to his outstretched chin.

Pohl fell back against the legs of a bystander, his own legs stretched out in front of him. The bystander kept him from going down until he moved, and Pohl found himself prone on the sidewalk. The big man pulled him off the ground and put him on his feet. Pohl got his balance and the man let go of him and stepped back.

"Fat clown," Pohl said, a thin ribbon of red going down his chin.

"Here?" the man asked.

"Right here," Pohl said, pointing his finger at the left side of his face.

The big man hit him with a short right to the jaw and caught him before he went down.

When he came to he was walking, or being dragged along the sidewalk by the big man. They came to an all-night café. He was put in a booth, and he sat upright with his head tilted back against the imitation red leather seat. A waiter came with a towel packed with ice and pressed it against his jaw. Pain shot upward through his head and played behind his eyes. Through the pain and involuntary tears he saw the big man standing behind the waiter with a fat hand on the booth. The big man looked worried.

Pohl forced a smile that hurt him. He didn't want the big man to feel guilty because he himself had forced the beating. There was a clock on the wall behind the waiter. He couldn't read it. He moved his head to get a look at it. The hands of the clock quivered in a veil of water that washed his eyes. Pohl took the towel from the waiter and thanked him. He held it against his own bruised chin. He asked for an iced soft drink and a straw.

The big man squeezed himself into the booth opposite Pohl and stared at his swollen face. He said he was sorry. He folded his hands on the tabletop and entwined his thick fingers. Pohl forced another smile. The big man kept his hands in front of him. The waiter came with Pohl's drink, the big man asked the waiter for a glass of beer. When the glass arrived he wrapped his big hands around it and swallowed several mouthfuls. He wiped the foam from his lips with the back of his hand. Pohl sipped his iced drink, he didn't hurry. It was sweet. The straw made it easier for him. The muscles of his face were sore. He'd got what he wanted. He thought of Angela only briefly between long periods of throbbing pain.

24

Violet reached up to the kitchen shelf for the box of powdered chocolate. She stood on tiptoe and the muscles of her calves stretched and rounded into a nice shape. She felt the muscles pulling all the way up her legs to her thighs and buttocks. She wanted to see what she looked like from behind. She knew it was a view that held them and spun them and made them dizzy, and there was no way around it. She used it whenever she got the chance because sooner or later she knew it would get her what she wanted and take her where she wanted to go.

She had thought that Burnett was it, that he was the destination. But she'd thought the same thing with several others. The box of powdered chocolate slipped out of her hand and tumbled off the shelf and she caught it. She took a carton of milk out of the refrigerator, the pan was already on the stove. She poured milk in it and lit the stove and waited for steam to rise up out of the lake of milk. Violet put two spoonfuls of chocolate in a cup, poured hot milk after them and stirred until it was cocoa-brown.

She took the cocoa to her bedroom, sat on the edge of the bed with her bare legs hanging down, her bare feet dangling above the floor. She switched on a lamp that was on the small bedside table and looked at the alarm clock. It was two-forty. She drank the hot chocolate, switched off the light. She tried to sleep but it didn't come because of the sugar in the cocoa and the thoughts in her head. She might not get what she wanted out of Burnett, and she needed the money. It was quiet in the room except for the ticking of the clock. Violet stretched herself and turned slowly in the bed and began a meditative scratching along the top of her head.

All the thinking in the world wasn't going to make any difference now. It wouldn't change a thing. She shut her eyes. She was on the fifth floor and she walked down the stairs very slowly, enjoying the feeling of going down one step at a time, lower and lower, no effort at all. Then she was asleep.

Burnett finished his whisky, the sky was growing dark beyond the windows of Angela's apartment while the big town lights came on and some of them winked at him through the Venetian blinds. Angela got up from her chair. She didn't have anything more to say to him. What came next was exactly what she knew he wanted her to do, and what she was going to do was what they'd agreed upon, and she breathed a sigh of relief because it was going to be her last performance. She left the living room and went to her bedroom to undress. She looked at herself in the mirror. She forced a smile and tossed her clothes on the bed. She was happy, if that was the word for it, that it was the last time she'd have to pretend that she wanted to play any game at all with Burnett. She might have enjoyed it with someone else, but it was just a means to an end with him.

Shimura looked through the stack of photographs Frankie Lundquist had left on his desk. They didn't tell him very much. Just that Burnett was looking at a lot of real estate in a lot of different locations with a city map in his hand and a handful of papers from a real estate agency. The photographs were crisp and clear, and the expensive lens Kawamura bought recently was evidently worth the price he'd paid. Still, he didn't see the point of pursuing Burnett, there was nothing unusual in his behavior, and he was losing interest in going after him for a woman like Violet, who he knew was hiding an ugly motive behind her request for an investigation into Burnett's comings and goings.

On the other hand, he was certain now that the man Violet was paying him to investigate and the man Pohl wanted to know more about were the same man. What was the connection? If there was a connection, what did it mean? The last print in the stack of photos was a shot of the street that ran in front of Burnett's building. It was night, and Shimura saw a woman's figure in a phone booth with the beams of a pair of headlights lighting her up.

Shimura searched his desk drawers for a loupe which, when he'd found it, he moved around on the photo in the area of the booth to get a better look at the figure inside it. Violet's features came into focus, but it didn't confirm a thing, he'd known all along that she would go on chasing Burnett because there was something big she wanted from him and she wasn't going to give up until she had it.

There was no wind at all and the rain falling from the sky had ceased to fall and the mists were rising from the warm earth. On his first day of going out to purposely observe the excesses of others, Aoyama made his way through a neglected garden strewn with rubbish, heading for the back door of a house he'd only just decided to enter when he made the decision to use it to get to the asphalt road on the other side. It was a technique he'd developed when he wanted to appear to others as if he had just left his own house by the front door so that it didn't look like he was snooping around a neighborhood he didn't belong to.

He wore a dreary gray sun hat and a holly-green, lightweight water-repellant coat. His brown leather boots crushed wet perennial grass, weeds, clover and wildflowers and patches of a kind of plant that spread by creeping rhizomes, scraps of plastic and pieces of paper with advertisements on them, rusted nails and tools, spent brass shells of ammunition, and the bent frame of a bicycle without handlebars.

He caught one of the heels of his boots in the bent, rusted spokes of a wheel and staggered clumsily forward until he regained his balance. Aoyama was short, with a flattish full face, thin lips, and a head covered by sparse black hair, crew cut, a scratchy voice.

He blinked, looking up at the two-story house divided into apartments like the other houses in the neighborhood that hadn't been torn down and replaced by soulless buildings. He climbed the ordinary wooden stairs, reached for the doorknob, turned it, and leaned weightlessly with his shoulder against the frame until it opened. He went in, shut the door noiselessly behind him. He stood for a moment, his eyes full of the damp gray morning.

He was in the kitchen. Coffee brewed in an automatic drip machine. His eyes followed the length of the horizontal countertop, went up the vertical line of the refrigerator, moved horizontally again along the rows of shelves with bright-hued cereal boxes and small packages closed with rubber bands, transparent and opaque bottles of olive oil and syrup and vinegar, powders and grains and spices that were ground, whole or pulverized. The slightly scuffed linoleum floor, red as a beet, wore signs of recent polishing. He gave everything the professional once-over without moving from the spot, then smiled.

Aoyama shut his eyes and breathed in the smell of coffee. A drop of sweat rolled down his nose and hung perilously at the tip. It tickled him. He wiped it away. The tickling sensation crept into his nose. He inhaled sharply, trying to stifle the sneeze he felt was coming. He pushed his tongue against the roof of his mouth. He shook his head, frowning. He looked up at the ceiling, concentrating on its pleasant whiteness. It's not the time, he told himself. The hairs in his nose trembled. He sneezed. Three times, and loud enough for anyone in the house to hear.

The phone rang. He heard footfalls coming toward the kitchen, didn't move an inch, and obeyed the steady-nerved signaling of his well-trained mind. He always kept a spare disguise in his pockets. He reached into one of them and pinched the molded plastic nose made by an expert and quickly fit it over his own nose. His other hand went to another pocket for a pair of black-framed glasses. He put them on the bridge of his plastic nose, shoved his sun hat into an empty pocket. His fingers found the flexible, rubberlike scalp with long, reddish hair and he fit it on his head, brushing strands of hair forward above his ears and backward on the top of his head. He wasn't working for the agency today, it was a day off, but he had his mind on the job at hand, and was always ready to refine his technique. His eyes purposely became shifting and beady, his expression falsely sinister, but relaxed.

A woman came into the kitchen, without seeing him, and went straight to the ringing phone. She answered it. She wore a floral-patterned dressing gown that looked like a worn-out satin bedcover. Aoyama looked at her bare feet and painted toenails. His eyes climbed the length of her body. She held the receiver between her tilted head and raised shoulder. She was slender, taller than Aoyama, like a stalk of tall treelike semi-tropical grass slightly bent, straining in the wind, and she was younger than him. She stood with her feet together, her eyes staring moodily at the floor, her lips firmly set, listening, with an impatient air, sighing heavily and just as heavily lifting her eyes, gazing off into space.

Aoyama couldn't breathe. It felt like cotton was packed tightly far down his throat, and that he was lying on his back under the rippling water of a river looking up at the woman's face. He shook his head to loosen himself from the grip of a kind of warning. He shut his eyes, the feeling went away. When he opened them, the woman was reaching out to shut off the coffeemaker.

She saw him when she turned her head, and she didn't look surprised. His face was hot. Her face was oval, pretty and pale. Her shoulder-length hair was neatly brushed and black, and she had a long neck. He thought: She must have a body that's not hard to look at poured into whatever she's wearing under that spread.

She waved the receiver at him, indicating a chair at the kitchen table. He took a few steps back, keeping his narrowed eyes on her, and sat down, crossing his legs like a dandy. He drew a pack of cigarettes out of a pocket. He lit up, exhaling a pleasant cloud of smoke and watched her through it. She gave him an exquisite smile. A drop of sweat as cold as mercury toiled down the nape of his neck, blotted itself into his collar.

She didn't remind him of any woman in particular except all the women he desired. She looked at him affectionately, returned to concentrate on whoever it was on the other end of the line. But he didn't trust her. It won't be long until she goes against me, he told himself. I'm just a clown that can smoke a cigarette. I don't belong here.

"No, Newton's not here," the woman said at last into the phone. "You really *are* observant, I've got to give you that."

Aoyama reached out for a grass-green ashtray and pulled it toward him, rolled the burning end of the cigarette gently on the rim, and a bit of ash came off. The woman listened to the voice on the other end of the phone.

"No, he couldn't. Because Newton's client didn't show up. He wasn't there. And you're right back where you started." She replied to words he couldn't hear. Her tone was aggressive. "Well, they were always afraid of everything, weren't they?" she went on. "What use have they ever been to him?"

Aoyama cleared his throat, the woman looked at him. He smiled apologetically, made a gesture with his hand at the pot of coffee. She nodded. Aoyama got up, looked around for a cup, the woman shook her head, cradled the receiver again, then opened a cupboard behind which half a dozen cups stood neatly in a row. She took hold of one of them and gave it to him.

He smiled weakly from the smell of her skin, an earthy humidity had seeped into his nostrils. He adjusted the glasses on his counterfeit nose. The cigarette hung loosely from a corner of his mouth and the smoke drifted upward past his eyes. He poured himself a cup of coffee, swallowed a mouthful and scalded his throat. It tasted so good that he almost forgot why he'd come to this house in the first place. The coffee gave him a feeling of kinship for the woman.

"When he gets back, I'll tell him. But don't waste your time calling here every ten minutes," she insisted. "Be patient. As far as it's within human capacity to be patient." She hung up.

Aoyama put his cigarette out, folded his hands on the tabletop. The chair was comfortable. He looked at the cigarette stub in the ashtray, then up at the woman, who steamily ran her tongue along her lips. She was playing a role, but he didn't laugh at her. Temptation, thought Aoyama. The skin tautened across her jaw and her face looked like a piece of pure, white marble, radiating a force that froze him in the chair. A chill crawled straight up his back and into the roots of his hair. She opened her mouth, her long white teeth sparkled.

She poured herself a cup of coffee, stirred three spoonfuls of sugar in it, making a tinkling sound with the spoon. His head bent low over the tabletop. The tinkling sound became a screaming noise and he shut his eyes. His brain turned a volume lever and made the noise many times softer than it really was. She stopped stirring. He raised his head, opened his eyes, and saw the woman put her cup down near his folded hands. She shrugged her shoulders, encouraging the dressing gown to slide down her back. She caught it with her slender fingers and draped it over the back of the chair opposite him. She gave Aoyama a bright smile.

She wore a sliplike undergarment made of silk that hung to the middle of her thighs. She sat down. Her arms were muscular. She turned her head slowly, forcefully to the left as far as she could, visibly straining her neck, and with the motion, the thin straps of the chemise rolled appealingly on her collarbone. She brushed her hand across her chest, wiping away invisible particles of dust, and her nipples almost pierced the plum-colored silk that clung to her pale skin. Aoyama's scalp started to itch beneath the latex stretched across his head.

"I don't know you," she stated flatly. She sipped from her cup, holding it steadily with both hands. "If you're looking for Newton, which I doubt, you're out of luck, and you already know he's not here. Unless you're deaf. In which case I've got to shout." She paused. "There's no one here but me. And that makes it convenient for you."

Aoyama swallowed another mouthful of coffee. He listened to her. He listened to people doing the talking because that's how he got the kind of information he needed for his job. He smiled sincerely at her. It's a good pitch, and I let her make it, he thought. But what she doesn't know would fill the Sea of Japan.

"I'm not here for Newton. I don't even know him. And I don't want to know him," he said calmly.

"No, maybe it's not convenient," she said. "I mean, not quite. It all depends on what you have in mind. I'm alone, attractive. Okay. Well, that leaves me on the spot. If you've got the nerve." She hesitated, leaning forward. "Have you got any?"

"Nerve? No use asking me," Aoyama said, twisting uncomfortably in his chair.

"If you try something, I won't yell. Not at all. If that's what's worrying you," she said contemptuously. "At least not until you're at it. And then it'll be strictly because I'm enjoying it. Just pleasure, that's me." She winked. "I want it, plenty."

She was looking at him through half-closed eyes, long eyelashes, and she sent him a dreamy smile. He knew now that he'd never forget her. A clattering noise came from the backyard. A piece of corrugated iron moved in a gust of wind. She didn't open her eyes for it, but cocked her head at the sound.

Aoyama knew what he was going to say and he said it: "Not a chance." Then he shrugged meaninglessly. "I'm not interested in what you want," he added, emphasizing each word.

She opened her eyes and fluttered her eyelids, and then her eyes were wide all of a sudden and brimmed with an exaggerated sincerity. "You don't care what you say to a woman, do you?" She looked young and untroubled. She stuck her chin out, highlighting the oval shape of her face. "You think you're tough." Now her teeth were clenched.

"Right now, no."

He felt his own pulse with two fingers, counted to himself, then reached for the pack of cigarettes, offered her one. She took it and fit it between her lips without opening her mouth. Her fingernails were the same color as the nails of her toes. Aoyama lit her cigarette, then his own. He sucked smoke into his mouth, filled himself up with the smoke and let it out between his teeth. The phone rang. This time she didn't answer it. She exhaled a cloud of smoke and looked at him with nymphlike eyes.

The phone stopped ringing, the wind stopped blowing, and the piece of corrugated iron didn't move or make a sound. He turned the cigarette between his thumb and forefinger and made it disappear like a magician. It reappeared between his lips. He squinted as the smoke trailed upward.

"I don't know whether to laugh or cry," she said, leaning forward with her elbows on the tabletop. "I'm telling you, I like it. I don't want you to refuse the offer. But as long as you're sure you don't want me, I won't make things any harder for you." She winked.

He looked down at himself and saw that his erect cock was trying to push its way through his trousers. His eyelids got heavy. There was a tense silence. She eyed him hungrily. He looked away, turning his head as if it had an enormous weight. Then he narrowed his eyes and stared back at her.

She was leaning back in the chair and playing indifferently with the plum-colored silk drawn tight across her breasts. She gave him a peculiar smile, put her cigarette out in the ashtray.

"I guess I feel kind of responsible for you now," she confided.

"That's obvious." He looked at the hill made by his erection. His head came up slowly, his eyes focused, and he said, "One of these days we'll get together on it, but not today."

"Not now, not ever." She smiled cheerfully. "You're not going to tell me you don't want it, are you?"

She reached up and pulled the left shoulder strap down past her upper arm. Her skin was truly pale, lightly freckled, and it shone in a ray of sunlight which came through the window and spread out harmlessly on the kitchen table just for the occasion.

Aoyama raised his brows and sighed heavily. His lips were numb just watching her. She pulled the other strap down and her breasts were exposed. She opened her mouth, a sparkle in her eyes, then sat up straight in the chair.

A drop of sweat squeezed out of his forehead and ran down the plastic nose. Warm rays of sunlight splashed on his face. A drawstring pulled in his throat. He was being pulled into nothingness. The sky, no matter how blue it was, lost its importance. The sheet of corrugated iron shivered. The structure of purpose inside his head fell apart, all the measured elements dropped away from his professional grasp.

The woman held onto the edge of her seat with both hands, swung her feet back and forth above the floor like a child, then inched the chair forward, making a dull scraping noise.

"Do you get what I'm saying?" she asked.

It wasn't really a question. He dug his fingernails into the palms of his hands. The drawstring jerked in his throat. His false nose started to slip down, oiled by perspiration and encouraged by the weight of his glasses. His right hand came up to put them in place. He tried to think of something to say. Aoyama inclined his head.

She gave him the answer herself. She grabbed a nipple between two painted fingernails, thumb and forefinger, and pinched hard. A flush shot upward under the surface of her skin. Her other hand stayed where it was, resting on her ribcage, and her fingers gave the same nipple another pinch, and this time she pulled it agonizingly upward and away from her body. Her eyes were very hungry. Aoyama winced. He stared at her tormented breast, then looked at her hair as a violent reddish-blue cast swept through it, engulfing her head like flames. Now her eyes were lit with a strange fire the color of fresh cucumber.

Aoyama fumbled in his pockets looking for his cigarettes. He found the pack, flicked his wrist to knock a cigarette out of it, put the wrong end between his lips, abruptly turned it around in his mouth with the filter now pressed against the tip of his tongue. He leaned anxiously forward and lit it, took several short drags, balanced it unceremoniously on the rim of the ashtray.

Her skin looked like transparent paper, the bluish veins were at the surface, wriggling like snakes. Aoyama trembled from head to toe. He took up the cigarette and inhaled and exhaled quickly until it was halfway smoked, then frantically put it out. He pressed his teeth into his lower lip. All the time the woman had been watching him and now she burst out laughing.

"Do you see my position?" she asked.

"What position is that?"

She tilted her chair back on its two rear legs, raised her own legs one at a time and propped her bare feet on the edge of the table. She parted her legs, moving her knees outward, and slowly pulled the hem of her chemise from her thighs to her waist. She wriggled around a bit to arrange it just right. She wore a pair of shiny, plum-colored panties that stretched tight across her lower belly below her navel at her hips. The panties showed a spot of moisture where her labia seemed to breathe like the mouth of a large fish. A few wiry pubic hairs poked anxiously out of the nearly transparent fabric. Aoyama averted his eyes after he got a good look at her.

"That's for you," she said, pointing at the wet spot with an accusing finger. She thrust her face forward, eyeing him. "Now, what becomes of the body after death?"

Her question frightened him. He aimed a level gaze at her. "You're not just leaking juice between your legs," he said.

She placed a finger to her lips, meaning silence. She stuck out her tongue menacingly. Her eyes were sometimes green, sometimes yellow. He might have jumped up and fucked her if he didn't know there was something wrong with her. She looked at him, pleading and reproachful. His cock strained against his trousers.

"You're a lot closer to it than you know," she said.

"To what, exactly?"

"Can't you smell it?"

Aoyama furrowed his brow, looked sideways at her. She ran her second finger up and down the wet spot.

"Looks like the question gives you more trouble than it gives me," she said.

"And what happens when you don't get what you want?"

"You'll find out." She sat up straight in the chair, opened her legs. "Most people can't even write their names properly when they get an eyeful of this." She placed the palm of her hand over her pussy, then slapped it. "And you're wasting your time talking."

He sat there a while silently nodding his head. He felt that time stood still, but the second hand on his wristwatch moved steadily forward. She looked bitterly at him, he gazed vacantly at her.

"As long as we breathe we can still change our minds," she said in a whisper. "Once upon a time there was a man named Aoyama."

"It's a circus here," he said. "How did you know my name?"

"I don't like you. But right now you're the man for me."

Aoyama smiled at something far away and that something smiled back at him.

"A virtuous man has been turned into a horse," he said.

"If anyone's interested, they can come and get you when I'm through with you and lock you up some place where you'll get plenty of oats morning and night." She raised her eyebrows comically. "If that'll make you happy."

"That's not exactly what I meant. You don't know the half of it."

"Half of what?"

He wanted to take her by the throat, by the hair, and smash her head into the refrigerator. And he still wanted to fuck her. He laughed voluntarily, too loud. He shifted a bit in his chair.

"You've got a lot of nerve." She giggled maliciously.

"Yeah."

"I'll tell you the half of it I know," she said. "You're going to forget whatever else it is you've got on your mind. You're going to concentrate on me because that's what I'm telling you to do. If you think you can do anything about it you're way off in some faraway place where there's no reality like the reality we've got here. It won't kill you. It'll probably do you some good. You don't have a clue about responsibility."

Her breath came and went like a ventilating system shuffling gusts of stale air.

"Just put it where it belongs," she went on. "Right here."

She slumped languidly in the chair, maintaining her balance, moved her knees farther apart, showing the taut muscles that were pulling on the inside of her thighs. They looked like something he could sink his teeth into. He wanted to do it right now. He wanted to swallow her. Just a bite. But she wasn't going to let go easily once she got hold of him. He showed his teeth in a grin, appreciating every inch of her. His eyes watered. His chin went up and down. She held him there. He didn't know how she was doing it. He almost wished Newton, whoever he was, was here.

"It doesn't make any difference what you think," he said at last. He looked down at his erection. Then his voice climbed an octave as he was saying: "No. None at all. No nerve. Zero."

"A man of genius gets drowned in his own talent," she stated flatly.

Aoyama looked away from her. He touched his face in various places. His nose hung down almost to his upper lip, his cheeks and neck were flushed. He straightened the nose and he straightened himself in the chair and he returned the woman's intense gaze. Say what you're thinking, he told himself. Say it. He opened and closed his mouth. But he wordlessly shrugged his shoulders. There was nothing he could say that would change anything.

She didn't laugh at him because he had nothing to say. A vein distended on her forehead with the seeming intention to burst. He narrowed his eyes and fidgeted in the chair, waiting for the spray of a ruptured vein. He snapped his mouth shut.

He felt like he weighed nothing at all. He shielded his eyes with his hands, then peered cautiously between his fingers. The features of her face were abnormally enlarged. The wet spot on her panties went on winking indecently at him. She opened her mouth, a bubble of saliva formed at the opening, and a strand of saliva dribbled out of it, streaming downward. When it touched one of her breasts it sizzled and evaporated from an intense heat.

At last, Aoyama stared at her in a wide-eyed daze. He saw her pale skin and hard bones under nearly transparent skin, a head of reddish-blue flames and a gaping red mouth that twitched violently, and the mouth offering him its sweetness was drawing him forward like a poisonous magnet. Not wanting to open his mouth, not wanting to kiss her, he opened his mouth. Not wanting to move, afraid of what she might do, he moved toward her.

She curled her painted toes around the edge of the table, her green eyes spun in their sockets. There was a strange light in them as if, in a trance, she were pursuing a dream. Aoyama snapped his mouth shut with all the force of a steam-shovel, then with a strength that surprised him he leaned back in his chair. Her gaping, watery mouth might have swallowed him. His lips curved up in a faint smile that contained both hope and anxiety. He swallowed hard, trying to get rid of the heavy thing in his throat.

It was now that he'd have to do something to put some distance between himself and the bitch with flaming hair and green eyes. He figured the moment was right because there wouldn't be another moment like it, and if he waited any longer he'd never get out of the house. Aoyama grabbed the edge of the table with one hand and shoved it just hard enough to knock the rear legs of her chair out from under her. She fell backward with the chair and landed with a thud on the linoleum floor, banging her elbows and the back of her head and letting out a shriek, cursing loudly.

He looked over the tabletop at her. He blinked, opened his mouth, held it open and closed it hard. The woman's hair was spread out around her head like a black sea and her head lolled on her bent neck. Strands of black hair were stuck together across her forehead.

"Maybe I don't know exactly why you're doing it," he said, "but I know what you want and you're not going to get it."

Her eyes focused, stared uncomprehendingly at him.

"That bothers me," she said.

"Bothers you?" He raised an eyebrow slightly. "I know what you are—an oracle of some things and not others."

"I can't stand arguments," she said. Her body gave a shudder, her mouth twisted and her eyes goggled.

He had nothing to say because he knew that he was right about her. He frowned, the frown became a grin, and he shrugged and said to himself: Maybe I'm right, but what does it matter?

"If only you'd been somebody else," she lamented while sprawled on the floor. Her chemise was twisted around her waist. "There's something heroic here between my legs!"

A voice came from him that wasn't his voice: "Where do you want it?"

He pressed his fingers against the bones of his face. He felt like laughing.

She let out a long sigh. She put out her tongue and licked her shoulder, then turned her gaze to him.

"I don't want anything from you," he said.

She propped herself on her bruised elbows.

"I want something from you."

"I want you to leave me alone."

"Quit worrying." The woman smiled.

"For the rest of my life I want you to leave me alone."

"The rest of your life is a matter of minutes if you don't fuck me," she said.

Bright red flowers blossomed and burned on her chest. He stared at the attractive patterns they made on her skin, then his eyes narrowed with disappointment.

"I hate to see a woman like you in a vulnerable position," he said, moistening his lips.

"Bring your face over here so I can smack it." She aimed a dim but dangerous smile at him.

Aoyama shook his head.

"Newton's not going to like it," she warned him.

"Fuck Newton."

"I already have."

He looked at the lustful expression on her face.

"What can I say after I say I'm sorry?" he said.

"You can tell me you want it, anyway."

"Who do you think you're kidding?"

"You're adding it up backward." She eased herself down taking the weight off her bruised elbows. Flat on her back, she stared at the ceiling.

"I know when I'm being kidded."

She said very quietly, "I want to keep you with me."

His eyes were dull, gazing past her. "You think you know me?"

She shook her head slowly. "You'll find what you're looking for but it won't be what you expected."

"Fortune-teller."

She didn't say anything.

Aoyama took a few steps backward without taking his eyes off her, then hurried out of the kitchen. He went quickly down the hallway toward the front door thinking about the road on the other side of it. It was the only reason he'd gone into this house in the first place, and it seemed now like one of the worst ideas he'd ever had. But the location was right for what he had to do. He wanted the anonymity it gave him.

No sound came from the kitchen to interrupt him. The woman had exhausted him and he felt how much his body was beat up. She'd given him a painful erection. He wasn't far from the door but he could have been a mile away. The hallway kept its low-ceilinged tunnel-like shape. He felt like an insect slowly being crushed between the pages of a book. His knees almost gave out. He groaned. He didn't know if he was going to make it. At last he pressed his hand against the smooth surface of the door, peered through the curtained window. The sun shone brightly between clouds from a distant patch of blue sky.

He grasped the handle and turned it and partly opened the door. He poked his head around it to check out Loomis Street for anything unusual, and he breathed in the fresh odor of the damp greens and fairways of a golf course a few blocks away.

"Good-bye!" the woman shouted grudgingly from the kitchen. "Stay alive and wait for me."

Aoyama jumped, he fumbled with the glasses and plastic nose and latex scalp. The disguise went into his pockets. He massaged his head, rubbed life back into his face, felt his heart bouncing around in his chest. He put the sun hat back on his head, swung the door open, and stepped out onto the porch. He looked like an ordinary resident of the neighborhood.

⸬ The door clicked shut behind Aoyama. He stood on the wooden porch and leaned against one of the stone pillars looking at the sidewalk and Loomis Street that shone with needless brilliance. His muscles tensed up. He looked sideways up and down the street past the wooden stairs a few feet in front of him. He looked at the sky where clouds refused to crowd out the sun. He squinted at the sunlight and at the reflection of sunlight in the upper windows of a house at the corner.

People came and went in a dreamy procession, walking in both directions along the sidewalk. Aoyama yawned, his jaw made a pleasant click in his head. Men dragged their feet in worn-out shoes, women held children's hands and mothers carried smaller children in their arms. Some people gathered at the bus stop, others went on walking on Loomis to the next intersecting street, turning there and following it to wherever they were going.

He lit a cigarette and exhaled a cloud of smoke that quickly blew away. He looked at the fronts of apartment houses that used to be plain, single family houses and the filthy doorways and the entrances scrubbed clean, windows open wide and shutters closed, a couple of air conditioning units that stuck out of a couple of lucky windows.

There was a four-story brick building up the street. A man stood framed in a window with a cup of coffee in his hand, looking at the morning sky and daydreaming and between sips he rubbed sleep from his eyes with a soft, barely awakened fist. In another window a woman studied her fingernails, then looked down at Loomis Street. In the window above her a man drank from a slim, half-pint bottle clasped in his hand. He wore a blank expression on his sleep-lined face.

The rearing outlines of roofs and chimneys slanted up against the sky. Television antennas and a few satellite dishes perched precariously on the roofs. A ruined two-story house leaned unhappily on its foundation like a block of Swiss cheese, with drill holes punched in the wood and pieces of plaster and brick cracked out of its ground floor walls.

Aoyama kept his head up, smoked indifferently while watching the street, looked like he was forming a mental picture of nothing. He squinted as a thread of smoke went into his eyes. He pinched the cigarette with his fingers and snapped it out in front of him. Okay, he said to himself.

He went down the wooden steps to the sidewalk, stretched, and looked up and down Loomis Street. A man came out of a dingy restaurant wiping eggs and coffee off his lips with his sleeve, then started whistling. Aoyama hated people who whistled as much as he hated people who sang to themselves. He wanted to kick the guy around the block. When they could see each other's face, the man gave him a warm and generous smile. Aoyama didn't hold the whistling against him.

He looked up at the few clouds that hung in the sky, weighty and confident like downy, feminine, lily-white buttocks. He wanted to squeeze them, but they were way out of reach like the pure, uninterrupted peacock-blue silkiness of sky spread out behind them. Aoyama brushed cigarette ashes off the sleeve of his raincoat, then started walking up Loomis past the two-story half-decaying house the color of broom-weed that showed plenty of partly exposed rusted iron rods in the fissures where crumbling walls had once been firmly joined.

28

The Venetian blinds in Shimura's office were raised on the garish neon of nighttime at twenty minutes after ten. Humidity streamed through the open windows on a breeze that ruffled a stack of papers on his desk.

Pohl sat in a chair facing Shimura, nervously tapping his fingers on the armrest. He puffed on a cigarette, turning its coal into an angry glow. A trail of smoke climbed in front of his eyes. Shimura put the phone receiver down, leaned back in his chair. He had an unlit cigar in his mouth.

"Another night, same thing. He's doing what he's done every night. Anyway, I've got someone following him until he goes home," Shimura said, trying to sound positive.

Pohl wasn't listening to him because the only thing he heard was a nagging voice in his own head that told him he'd never have a chance to tell Angela how much he loved her and that he might as well throw himself out of a window.

"She hasn't answered the phone for a week," he said, putting a whine into his voice. "I want to marry her, Shimura. I want the same thing Kawamura's got with Asami. Just like you told me. Why can't I have what Kawamura has?" He pulled at the cigarette. "You've got to find her."

"There's nothing on Burnett that puts him with Angela, not now, not anymore," Shimura explained.

"Tell me, again."

"A witness, a woman who lives in the same building as Angela, saw Burnett on more than one occasion enter the building and climb the stairs to Angela's floor. We showed her two photographs of Burnett. The woman confirmed it. She lives on the floor below Angela, and she crossed him on the stairs going up, she waited, looked through the banister, saw him at her door, heard him knock at the door and saw Angela open it."

Pohl nodded, crushed his cigarette in the ashtray. The breeze blew smoke back in his face. He got up, paced back and forth in the small office spending more time avoiding furniture than walking in a straight line. He stopped behind the chair he'd been sitting in. He gripped the glistening black wood.

Nothing happened. Pohl just stood there, his face pale and expressionless in the glow of lamplight.

Shimura forced a smile. He didn't know what to tell him because there was nothing to say that would ease the pain. He wanted to help Pohl, they'd been friends for a long time. He wasn't going to argue about whether or not Pohl's idea of marrying Angela was a good idea or had anything to do with reality, or if Angela, on her side of it, was even considering marriage.

"Finally, I made up my mind," Pohl said, "and now she's gone."

Shimura nodded. "Sit down, Burt."

"So it was Burnett who was with her the night I showed up and she wasn't alone," Pohl said. "Well, just tell me one thing. Do I have to put up with it?"

"He hasn't seen her in more than a week."

Shimura reached for a thermos of black tea. He poured a cup and offered it to Pohl.

"I made the identification for you," he said. "It was Burnett, but now he's out of the picture. Leave it alone, Burt — for your own good."

Pohl didn't see the cup of tea because his eyes were staring out the window at the skyline. His mind was racing but he wasn't in gear. And then, his voice low, the words coming slowly, he said: "All right, that's one thing. And the other is what's happened to her."

The phone rang. Shimura put the cup of tea down and picked up the receiver. He listened without saying anything. Pohl fingered another cigarette but didn't light it. Shimura cradled the receiver, poured himself a cup of tea, sipped it, kept on listening. Pohl's complete attention was on Shimura.

Shimura's tone was technical as he said: "Did you do what I asked you to do?" He paused. "Okay. That's right. Go on home."

He hung up, took another sip of tea, put the cup down. He leaned back in the chair, pushed it away from the desk, crossed his legs and folded his arms.

29

Violet got out of the taxi and went straight for the doors of the hotel bar on upper Jackson Street. There were people walking in both directions on the sidewalk past the entrance through the glow of streetlights, and some of them turned their heads to look at her. She walked that better-than-average walk swinging her narrow hips enough to make her skirt ripple like water in a breeze. The door swung shut behind her. Just after the checkroom she stopped and looked around the bar as the waiters and barmen smiled and nodded at her.

She went over to an empty, burgundy leather armchair at a low, round table and sat down facing the bar. She was going to wash away her Burnett troubles with a lot of alcohol. She crossed her legs slowly, deliberately, and the skirt slid up her thigh. A waiter brought her a lemon vodka and ice.

There were seven low, round tables in the room, a lucky number for the house, and five barstools at the bar. Four tables were occupied, three barstools had customers sitting on them. Seven, again. She shut her eyes while she took a sip. Lemon vodka and ice felt cool moving down her throat. She opened her eyes. The walls and ceiling and furniture were mahogany. The room was softly lit by wall sconces that pointed their warm flamelike bulbs at the ceiling.

The dining room adjacent to the bar was half-filled, a jazz trio played out of a corner to the clatter of knives and forks on porcelain. A waiter carried a tray of drinks from the bar to the dining room. Violet sipped her vodka, fingered the hem of her skirt. Her head was down but her eyes looked furtively at the customers at the bar.

Her upward gaze caught the back of a man's head just above his neatly shaved neck. That was a start, the shaved neck was clean, there was plenty of messy blonde hair above it, and she liked the shape of his head. The sting of her gaze made him turn around. He looked at the woman whose eyes bored into him.

Violet saw the soft gray eyes in the soft light because there was some kind of glow behind them that shone at her. His shoulders were broad but he wasn't a wide man. He wore a gray suit with a vertical suggestion of violet, a white shirt with an open collar. He pushed his hand through his hair, turned his back to her.

A cigarette burned in the ashtray in front of him. He put it between his lips and took a drag, crushed it out. His glass was empty, he ordered another drink from the bartender, who poured a whisky with ice and set it down on the bar in front of the man. He stared blankly at the cracked ice floating in the whisky, raised the glass and took a mouthful of it. Then he felt the heat again at the back of his neck from a pair of eyes across the room. He swung around on the barstool and his mouth was curved in a smile and his gray eyes were very hot and intent. He met the gaze of the woman staring at him.

He extracted a cigarette from the pack on the bar and lit it. He inhaled deeply, blew a cone of smoke at the mahogany ceiling. He climbed off the barstool with the drink in his hand and went to the table where the woman sat looking up at him. Half her face was in shadow, but the half he saw told him he'd like how all of it would look in full light. And there was the way she was eyeing him.

Violet uncrossed her legs, scratched the skin under the hem of her skirt, and inched the skirt further up her thighs. She kept her eyes fixed on the man standing in front of her. She liked how he looked at her. And so that was it. She nodded emphatically. He sat across from her at the low, round table. It was just as clear and simple as that.

30

Pohl left the building with Shimura. At the exit they said goodnight. Shimura turned to the right and headed for his car. Pohl stood still, listening. He heard Shimura start his car in the vacant lot alongside the building. He frowned, thinking of Angela. His bladder felt like it was going to burst from all the black tea he'd drunk with Shimura.

The headlights of Shimura's car swept out into the street on the downtown emptiness of night. Pohl wanted to pull the mild night calm down deeply to his lungs but his worrying got in the way, and he turned left and walked gloomily down the sidewalk through evenly spaced circles of light cast by streetlamps. There was a bus stop a few blocks away. He walked slowly, hesitantly toward it, but he really didn't feel like going home and he wanted the walk to last as long as possible.

He came to a karaoke bar and went in, walking the length of it to the back where there was a toilet and a public phone. He let out a sigh while he emptied his bladder, then in front of the mirror he looked at himself. He put his fingers gently against the healing bruises on the left side of his face where the big man's fist had crashed into him. The beating had taken his mind off Angela for about an hour, and by the time he'd taken the ice pack out of the freezer at home he was at it again, worrying.

There weren't many people at the bar. The bartender was dozing standing up. Pohl didn't order a drink. No one even looked at him as he moved past them to the door and walked out. He went on past the bus stop. The street was almost empty. His mood was a mixture of sadness and anger. He didn't believe that Burnett was out of it no matter what Shimura had said. He couldn't stop all the questions swimming around in his head. He was fed up with himself. He shut his eyes, trying to erase some of it from his mind. He opened them, winced and stiffened. He crossed the intersection, went on walking. Then he thought of Violet.

He didn't know her, but he'd learned enough from Shimura to know that she was an irresistible force that made things difficult for anyone who got in her way, and he began to wonder whether or not Angela had been an obstacle and if Violet was somehow involved in the fact that he didn't have word from Angela for days, and he wondered if Violet thought Burnett was serious about Angela.

Maybe Angela was serious about Burnett. He hadn't thought of that. Pohl shook his head, his stomach was tied up in knots. But his mind took it further than competition between two women for a man and finished with an ugly picture of Violet taking Angela out of this world. Now he really wasn't feeling very good with the taste of death in his mouth. Violet might have killed her. He was chasing after some kind of logic and what he'd come up with didn't make any sense to him.

His mouth clamped shut, he went on walking until he tripped on the uneven sidewalk. Pohl smiled. He leaned against a lamppost and lit a cigarette. He stood there watching the street, the people, the cars, and a late-night bus pull away from the curb. He took a drag on the cigarette. He went on dragging at it until it was down to a stub, hurled the stub to the sidewalk and stepped on it.

The bar where he'd gone to urinate, the street where he'd tripped on the sidewalk, and the last cigarette he'd smoked were far behind him now because he was making his way down Prospect, heading toward Angela's place, with her apartment house not far away on Lake Street in the shadowy places between streetlights.

Pohl found a suitable doorway, stepped into its darkness and leaned against the protruding edge of the doorframe, waiting. He watched the entrance of Angela's building, knowing it was useless to wait for her because she'd disappeared but so determined to see her that what made sense for someone else didn't matter to him. He lit a cigarette. He was going to wait until the sky brightened enough to tell him to go home.

Shimura turned the steering wheel to the right, brought the car to the curb. He was a half-block from where he lived on Ruby Avenue. He walked to the all-night corner market at Ruby and 12th. There was a middle-aged man with dark skin and dark hair and bright brown eyes and a beer bottle in one hand, standing in front of the vegetables laid out in rows next to the refrigerator filled with bottles of sparkling water, fruit juice, soda and ice-cold beer. Shimura opened the glass door and picked up two bottles of sparkling water.

The middle-aged man gathered handfuls of green beans and dumped them in a plastic bag and tied the bag shut, counted out a half-dozen carrots and dropped them in another bag, then selected four ripe tomatoes. He picked up a box of macaroni. Shimura watched him out of the corner of an eye, paid for the bottled water, added some change for a late edition newspaper and stood in front of the market looking at the front page.

What he read said nothing new to him, there was nothing new to tell in the world, now as then, except maybe the location was new, where something happened, or the people involved in what happened were different people, and whatever was behind it all, one way or another, the reason was always the same, it was just one thing, and it would always be just one thing, and that one thing was really two things rolled into one, the most important of them was money, and the other was sex. Shimura looked up from the newspaper at the man leaving the market with his macaroni, vegetables, and a bottle of beer.

Pohl looked down at the dozen cigarette butts at his feet. He pushed them with the edge of his shoe, stepped out of the doorway to the sidewalk and started down the street. He looked over his shoulder at the entrance to Angela's building. A taxi pulled up, a man got out and went into the building. There had been no sign of Angela. A van delivering dry cleaning turned the corner in front of Pohl. He thought about sleep. At last he was looking forward to going home.

A battered red car was parked every night in front of his apartment building on Fourteenth Street and he saw it now as he wearily rounded the corner. At the same time he spotted the car he saw the man he'd collided with the night he'd seen Angela perform for Burnett.

The man walked along the sidewalk on the opposite side of the street. Pohl crossed the street, moved slowly toward him. The early morning light poured lavender into a yellowish-gray sky. The man was smoking a cigar. He came to a stop in front of Pohl, who stared at him. The man wore a loose, turquoise-blue silk shirt that hung over the waistband of his wide trousers. He looked Pohl up and down, smiled at him as he chewed on the end of the cigar. Thick smoke swirled up in front of his face. Pohl couldn't swallow the coincidence.

"This tickles me," the man said. "It's really funny."

"I don't want to know anything." Pohl was cautious.

"So, we meet again," the man stated flatly.

"No objection?" Pohl remembered the words the man had said the first time they'd met.

"Know where I've been?"

"Not again. Don't tell me," Pohl said.

"It's what I like to do."

"I asked you politely."

"I work a lot," he confided. "I spend my money the way I want to spend it."

"That's not my business."

"Fucking is the best thing I can think of doing." The man exhaled a cloud of smoke, grinning. "I've got the right to do it because I've got the money to pay for it."

Pohl turned away from him, crossed the street, heading for the battered red car. He leaned against the fender, stared at nothing. The man followed him, stood in front of him, waved his hand in front of Pohl's face.

"I was just fucking," the man said. "Nobody's going to bite you. We're having a conversation. Do you hear me?"

Pohl snapped out of it, his gaze with a parade of questions in his eyes returned to the man in front of him.

The man's face glowed with a healthy complexion, the cigar stuck straight out of his mouth between thick, pinkish lips. A smile worked its way onto the lips, a perceptive smile that narrowed his eyes.

"Let me answer one of them."

"One of them, what?" Pohl asked.

"Questions."

Pohl blinked, folded his arms across his chest and stared straight ahead.

"I'm here to tell you all your worrying is for nothing," the man said. "Fucking is what you want. It's the solution to everything."

Pohl opened his mouth to say something, and his mouth stayed open, but no sound came out. The man reached out, put a warm, human hand on Pohl's shoulder, then turned and walked away. A cloud of cigar smoke trailed up over the man's head. Pohl looked at it, and it told him there would be trouble if he didn't find Angela because she was the fire that got him going and he was the smoldering smoke that came from it, and without her he didn't exist. He pushed away from the red car, went to the entrance of his building, opened the door and let it swing shut behind him.

33

Shimura sat in the kitchen with a glass of sparkling water and ice, looking at his small, almost feminine hands spread out on the tabletop in front of him. He heard the clock above the kitchen sink ticking off the time. It was late. There were no other sounds in the building.

Professional necessity had given him the ability to turn his eyes without the use of his head and he did this while he sat at the table taking an occasional sip of water. His eyes caught something like the presence of Burt Pohl. Other than that, whatever he saw was familiar and it meant everything and nothing to him because he'd been looking for a long time at what he had and where he lived. He was used to seeing all of this but not, out of the corner of his eye, the presence of Pohl without Pohl really being in the kitchen with him.

What he saw wasn't really Pohl, of course, but it was the worrying Pohl was giving him because worrying was just as much a part of friendship for him as honesty or brotherhood. A friend like anyone else was capable of making a mistake or losing his power of reason over a woman, and it was his duty to worry about it and maybe do what he could to bring that power of reason back to Pohl.

He might have wanted the same thing for Pohl that Kawamura had with Asami, but they were entirely different stories and he couldn't substitute one for the other. Angela herself didn't know what she wanted. It was trouble no matter which way he looked at it. He'd told Pohl what he knew about Burnett, but the facts weren't enough to dissuade him from wanting to find her. Maybe what he called worrying was only thinking.

Shimura got up from the kitchen table, finished his glass of water and left it in the sink. He left his conscience, and the presence of Pohl behind him because he wanted to get some sleep. The rest of the apartment was in darkness. He went down the short hallway past the bathroom to the bedroom and his fingers automatically found the light switch. He was asleep not long after he'd undressed, brushed his teeth and washed his face and hands.

34

Violet's green eyes opened and she stared up at the ceiling, breathing in and out, and it was almost like a sigh of relief. The corners of her mouth moved up, starting to build a smile. There was a downy pillow under her head and someone breathing evenly beside her. She turned to look at the man that had been wearing a gray suit with a vertical suggestion of violet. Now she was horizontal and he was sound asleep. His hair hung lazily across his forehead.

Violet had heard what she wanted to hear him tell her in the hotel bar. He was good-looking and soft-spoken, and he had plenty of money and no family to take it away from him. And she thought: Nobody to take it away from me if I ever get my hands on it. In the hotel room they fucked and liked it, and so they did it again and again, and it was not at all bad for a first time. She knew that the feeling would improve each time they did it, and it would no longer be fucking and then it would be called making love. But that was only if she went on seeing him and if he wanted to see her, and at this moment she didn't know what was going to happen between them.

She went over it in her mind. She was already making plans. He was going to be a lot better for her than Burnett and so she decided right then to forget about him. She'd call the Kawamura Agency and tell Shimura that she didn't want anything from Burnett, he could drop it, and she'd pay him for his time. She was going to let Burnett off the hook even though the idea of it made her stomach turn. But it was going to be worth it. This one was a gold mine. She'd made a mistake thinking so small and ignoring the fact that she was lucky more than once in her life and figuring that Burnett was the limit when this man lying next to her now was proof that there was no limit.

The man made a smacking sound with his lips. She didn't like it but she could live with it because it came with money and fucking.

She wiggled her toes. She inched closer to him, felt his breath on her face. She wanted to know what he was like in the morning. He had long eyelashes. She stuck her tongue out and ran it over the short, rough growth of beard. He mumbled a few words, his eyelashes fluttered and his eyelids raised halfway. She snuggled against him, tucked her face into his armpit and smelled him. She concentrated deeply on the smell and felt a wetness build between her legs. She reached down and held his cock in the palm of her hand. She stroked it, pulled it toward her, pumping it until it got hard.

35

On the second day of his research into the excesses of the city's inhabitants, and his search for Angela Mason, Aoyama looked up at the yellow-complexioned sunlight that came down hard on the pavement, drank in the sunlight because the sunlight was strong like the persuasive warm-blooded halo of love, and breathed the air slowly to find out if he could already taste the gritty pollution in it.

He went through his pockets looking for the photograph of Angela Mason that Shimura had given him. She'd gone missing, but when they located her, he was going to be in on it as soon as they got her out of whatever it was she'd got herself into. He examined her face, gazing closely at her bright eyes. A lot of people have it worse than you do, and there are thousands of people who have it worse than the people who have it worse than you. He sighed, put the photograph back in his pocket. Aoyama turned left on Kenton Street.

Aoyama continued along the sidewalk following Kenton with his raincoat over his arm. Thoughts came to him that were all sizes and colors, but at the heart of them today was Angela Mason. He'd found a lot of missing people in a lot of different circumstances through the years at the Kawamura Agency. The pictures of them rolled around in his mind, playing like a lot of choppy films. He slipped a frame of Angela into the stream of pictures.

As he saw it, a vision or a kind of second sight, her restrained, pale body was elastic in spite of itself. She was tied with rope to the plumbing under the sink in a dingy bathroom of a broken-down apartment where the toilet was filled to overflowing with shit. Her large sea-blue eyes were almost completely extinguished by the hours and days she'd spent waiting for someone to find her. The ropes were slackened from her pulling at them. Whoever had tied her up had tied the last knot and left her there with a bare 60-watt bulb burning in a fixture above the sink. Water dripped from the faucet. Her legs were bent at the knees and tied together with a rope attached to her ankles. Her feet arched in a spray of light stretching out across the filthy bathroom floor.

Aoyama came to a halt at the corner of Monroe Street and Kenton, lowered his head. He'd been thinking in typical Aoyama-fashion, and he wasn't surprised that he'd suddenly become depressed. He looked up at the sky, where he saw Angela Mason's face through a sort of filter, like a thin photographic slide placed against his retinas, and it wouldn't go away.

36

Shimura hung up the phone and got up from the edge of his desk. Violet had just saved him the trouble of closing out the account she'd opened on Burnett. He'd already decided the investigation was going nowhere and that she could hustle Burnett herself without wasting his time. He didn't want any part of a paycheck that came from a woman like her. But she'd played an important role by inadvertently giving him a connection between Burnett and Angela. From what he knew, Burnett hadn't seen Angela in over a week and there was nothing to add to that fact.

He went to Kawamura's office. The door was open, and Asami, wearing large round glasses, was standing next to Kawamura with the double-paned windows behind her. The daylight made them shapes without faces. Kawamura looked up at him, smiling. Asami bowed her head, brushed past him. Shimura went in, shut the door behind him.

Kawamura couldn't keep from grinning. "The wedding is in two months," he said.

Shimura bowed. "I wish you every happiness. A man is always lucky when he's going to be married, Kawamura-*san*," he said, looking down at Kawamura. "I put Aoyama on the missing woman." It was a half-truth because he was using Eto and Frankie, too.

Kawamura was shuffling papers on his right. "I *will* be very happy." When he found what he was looking for he wrote something in the upper right-hand corner, then dropped it on a pile of papers to his left.

Shimura turned around and headed for the door, but before he had his hand on the doorknob he heard Kawamura say: "I'm letting you use him because Pohl's your friend and you're willing to deduct the costs from your salary."

"I know that, Kawamura-*san*." Shimura didn't turn around.

"But there's a limit to how long I'll let you use him."

Now he did turn around, bowed slightly. "Thank you, Kawamura-*san*."

He shut Kawamura's door behind him, turned and smiled at Asami, sitting at her desk, walked past her, rubbing his chin thoughtfully, and left by the front door.

37

It was afternoon, and Burnett lay stretched out on the sofa in his pajamas. He rubbed his thigh through the silk trousers, stared at the ceiling with a blank look on his face. He was thinking of a lot of things and nothing at all. There hadn't been any news from Angela for nearly a week, she'd dumped him. He might've taken it a step further with her, but when it was done it was really done, and if he'd had any news it wouldn't have mattered because he was already bored with her, her usefulness had come to an end, and he'd started proceedings for a replacement. A friend of his named Cooper had introduced him to a young black woman, Cathy Jones, who worked at the cosmetics counter of a department store downtown, and they'd had a drink together in the bar at the Regent Hotel.

Now he had nothing better to do than think about the women he'd seen and didn't know or knew and hadn't yet started anything with and what he'd like to do with them, and he wondered if they'd go as far as Angela had gone. He had left a message on Cathy Jones' answering service. Her particularly smooth skin made his cock hard. He wanted her to call him. He stretched his arms and folded his hands behind his head.

Then he had a flash of Violet. He stayed with it. Much to his surprise, she had gone off the map, not the way Angela had, but in her own way, with a few lousy insults on the phone. No more calls, no surveillance, no unannounced visits. It was a relief. But he had a panicky feeling that he was being watched. He thought he had seen a woman with unnaturally white teeth chewing gum in a car parked across the street.

The blinds were drawn and the room was in semi-darkness. A round spot of sunlight crept across the wall opposite him. He reached out for a toothpick resting on the edge of an empty plate with cracker crumbs and a remnant of the creamy center and whitish rind of Camembert.

The telephone rang. It was Cathy Jones.

"I'm ready," Cathy said. Her voice whispered in his ear.

"I guess you are." Burnett switched the phone to the other hand and put his index finger in his ear where her voice tickled him.

"Tell me what to do," she said.

"You're in a hurry, and that's not good. This is the kind of thing we've got to take our time with, to enjoy it, I mean."

"Okay, whatever you say. Just explain it to me."

"Don't worry about that, I'll tell you everything. You're not old enough to know about things like that anyway, and I want you to like those things as much as I'll like doing them with you."

"Maybe I *do* know what you're talking about, Lew."

"You do? Maybe you don't."

He put the phone back against the ear she'd tickled with her voice.

"I'm ready, when you are," she said.

"I want you to wear a skirt, just above the knees, not too short. No stockings, I want your black legs and black feet bare. Low-heeled shoes, or sandals. I want to see the upper parts of your toes. Wear dark-blue panty briefs. A shirt with buttons, no bra. Do you have a plastic raincoat? Wear it. Go to a sex shop. Buy a vibrator, a kind of egg with a remote control. Don't forget the batteries. At the sex shop, put the vibrator inside you. Switch it on. Find a taxi. In the backseat, cross and uncross your legs. Make sure you're good and wet. Do you have something to write with? I'll give you my address."

38

A faint rustling noise above him made Aoyama turn his head. He heard it again and looked up. A man wearing pajamas was leaning out of a window past a window box full of flowers. He was craning his neck, looking to the left and right. Aoyama crossed to the other side of the street to watch him. The man left the window frame for an instant and came back with a small watering can which he waved in a sweeping motion above the flowers. Then he disappeared from view again. Aoyama stepped back into a doorway out of the way of pedestrians. It looked like a gaseous cloud hung over the flowers.

The man returned to the window, stood in front of the bright-hued flowers holding a cigarette lighter. Aoyama squinted. The man lowered his arm, turned his wrist so that the fingers grasping the lighter were just above the flowers. He struck the wheel with his thumb and a flame leapt quickly up from the window box. He jerked his hand away from the spreading flames, stepped back to admire his handiwork, dropped the lighter into the shirt pocket of his pajamas.

He saw Aoyama watching him from a doorway on the opposite side of the street. He cupped his hands around his mouth.

"I can't help it!" he said hoarsely and loudly.

Aoyama shook his head. The flames moved along the length of the window box. The flowers were gone, and the man laughed a hard, dry laugh, hopped up and down, showed his teeth with a broad smile, and his eyes screwed up like he'd just had an orgasm.

The window box caught fire. The man was in a state of ecstasy and didn't see how far the thing had gone. He was a fire bug and when the craving came it hit him so hard that he couldn't wait to get started and getting it started required immediate action, now it was going to be a bigger fire than he'd bargained for, something on the order of three alarms, because the wooden box trimmed with metal was dry and a lot like kindling, and the wood frame building was old and dry and he was too busy with the pleasure he got from looking at the flames to notice it.

Aoyama was already taking the stairs two at a time in the old building, holding on to the railing and moving as fast as he could to get to the man's apartment before the fire got out of hand. He didn't knock at the door but threw himself against it and it swung open right away.

The man was sitting in an armchair staring at the burning window box with his arms folded and a blank expression on his face. Aoyama ran down the short hallway and found the bathroom, grabbed a bath towel, threw it in the sink and turned on the faucet.

The towel soaked in water left a trail at Aoyama's feet as he hurried to the window with it. He spread his arms holding the corners of the towel and dropped it on top of the window box over the flames.

39

Shimura crossed the street to the newsstand. He picked up a daily and dropped a coin into the palm of the news dealer's hand. He went around to the other side of the newsstand, stood in front of a wall of advertising posters, opened the newspaper to the city section and searched the columns. He wasn't looking for anything in particular. It was ten minutes after nine. He folded the newspaper, turned away from the newsstand.

In the corner restaurant, he found a small red leather booth for two and sat down to wait for Pohl. He'd talked at length with Hadley about what he was going to say. He ordered a glass of tomato juice with Worcestershire and Tabasco sauce and celery salt. The waiter left it in front of him. He used the spoon to fish the slice of lemon from the bottom of the glass, squeezed the lemon juice into the drink, wiped his hands on a napkin. He took a sip, squinted down at the glass as if it tasted badly, then downed half of it, exhaling the flavor. He went on reading the newspaper.

At a few minutes before ten a taxi let Pohl out at the corner in front of the restaurant. Shimura watched him pay the driver and almost collide with a couple waiting in line at the movie theater. He went back to the newspaper. Pohl swung the restaurant door open, spotted Shimura, made his way past the tables and the people sitting at them until he stood over Shimura, who was looking at the personals and shaking his head. He pointed out a notice to Pohl, who leaned over his shoulder to read it:

> *looking for a honest, sweet guy treat me right. i don't have*
> *any bf or friends*

Pohl sat down, Shimura set the folded newspaper on the tabletop, stared thoughtfully at Pohl. The waiter came to the table, Pohl ordered a beer, the waiter returned with an ice-cold bottle of beer and a glass.

They raised their glasses, each thinking in terms of friendship, and the benefits that it brought, and the comfort of being a man with friends, and what it meant in a city where a majority of people thought only of themselves and what they got out of life.

"I'm late. Sorry," Pohl said.

"You're here."

"That's right."

"And you're looking okay."

"I'm feeling okay. Better."

Shimura drank from his glass.

"I want you to know that whatever was going on between Angela and Burnett, it's finished," he said. "Over and done. And he's not worth wasting your time."

Pohl looked at him and into him and said: "I've already come to the same conclusion. I've already given up on it. On the idea of doing something to him, I mean. I don't care." He swallowed a mouthful of beer. "I just want Angela."

"I know you do."

Shimura finished the Virgin Mary, waved the waiter over to the table.

"You want another?"

"No, thank you," Pohl said. He lit a cigarette.

Shimura ordered another Virgin Mary.

"You're my friend," he said.

"I know that."

"I'm thinking about Angela."

"So am I."

"Not like that. I mean, what are you doing?"

"What do you mean, what am I doing?"

"She's not for you. She may be your type, but she's not for you. If it's sex—"

"Listen—"

"No, you listen. What are you thinking?"

"That's a lot of questions you're asking me."

"I'm a detective." Shimura suppressed a smile.

"Funny."

"Okay. What I'm going to do now is find her for you, then it's up to you how to handle it."

The waiter put the glass of tomato juice in front of Shimura, who stirred the concoction of Worcestershire and Tabasco sauce and celery salt with a spoon, fished out the lemon slice, put it in his mouth and sucked on it. The waiter replaced the used ashtray with a clean one. Pohl stubbed his cigarette out in it.

"If you want to marry her," Shimura said, "I'll fix it so that you can ask her to marry you because I'll find her."

"I'm in love with her."

"You're infatuated. A crazy, one-sided infatuation. That's what it is, and you know it."

"You want me to change my mind? Why do you want me to do that?" Pohl threw his arms out in a confused, somewhat frantic gesture.

"I'm trying to tell you how it really is," Shimura said solemnly.

"I don't even hear you."

"You hear me and you know it's the truth. You have no argument. But I promised you and you can hold me to it."

Pohl didn't answer, he lit another cigarette and moved the idea of Angela around in different parts of his mind looking for a place where she really fit in and when his doubts about her rose like a black storm cloud, he waved them off. He gave Shimura a slow smile.

"I know I've got it coming, what you're telling me," Pohl said, "and I know that you're saying it for my own good, but I'm not going to give up just like that." He looked at Shimura and didn't have to force a smile.

"What you want from her isn't something you're going to get, but you'll have to find that out for yourself." Shimura drank from his glass of tomato juice.

Pohl took a long drag at the cigarette. As the smoke came from his lips, he said: "What can I do?"

"Nothing. Leave it to me."

Pohl waved at the waiter, who took his time making his way through the restaurant to their booth, and when he got there he took Pohl's order, poured the contents of the half-empty bottle into Pohl's glass. Pohl drank it down. When the waiter returned with another full bottle of ice-cold beer Pohl didn't touch it.

"I know her, and I don't know her," Pohl said at last. "I haven't figured it out. Maybe I can't see it because I'm in love with her."

"Maybe I can't see anything without an angle if that's what I'm looking for," Shimura said.

"We'll find out."

"Do you think she's in trouble?"

"No." Pohl raised his glass of beer to his lips.

"That's what I think, too."

"Then what is it?" Pohl asked helplessly.

"If I knew that, well, it'd be a lot easier for both of us."

40

Rand Hadley crossed the park away from its western edge bordered by the river, on freshly mowed grass, and the short green blades wet with dew moistened his shoes. Shimura sat on a wooden bench at the edge of the park facing the parkway, reading the morning edition. The sun shone brightly from a cloudless sky. The flow of cars on the parkway was like a soft-distant murmur in Shimura's ears.

Hadley swung wide and came to the bench on Shimura's right so as not to startle him by coming up to him from behind. Shimura folded the paper on his lap, wiped the bench seat with his handkerchief, and Hadley sat down.

"Any news from your ex-wife?" Shimura asked.

"I had her on the phone the night before last and we've worked it out. I'll add something to the monthly payment, and she'll get some overtime."

"You're lucky, Rand. Even divorced, you're lucky."

"You don't have to tell me."

Hadley took a pack of gum out of his pocket, offered a stick to Shimura, who refused it with a smile.

"Disgusting habit," Hadley said, then unwrapped a stick and put it in his mouth.

"There are times I wish for a special kind of surgery, like an operation that would get rid of emotions."

"You're wrong. It's just the thing that gives you an edge if you don't let it get to you," Hadley said, chewing slowly with his mouth shut.

"Pohl's acting just like a kid by chasing after a woman who's about as well-balanced as somebody falling off a building. I wonder if finding her is really doing him a favor."

"If you lose your head over that—"

"I won't lose my head, Rand. And I'm going to find her. That's what's bothering me."

"Part of a day's work."

"He'll be worse off with her around."

"You can't please everybody. Especially when you're a cop."

"You're telling me. It's the same with detectives at the agency."

"When you're a cop, you'll be criticized, no matter what you do. My advice to you is to stop cracking yourself on the head, take off the brass knuckles and go easy. You'll get enough to sweat about from everybody else."

"And then I think of all the cases I've worked on, and I get very tired."

"We all get tired."

"I guess I'm making a big thing out of nothing."

"You're doing what you can do for a friend."

41

Shimura stretched out his legs and crossed his ankles. The television was on with the sound switched off and the remote control lay next to him on the small sofa. He held a glass of sparkling water against his chin, staring at nothing, then put it to his open mouth and swallowed a mouthful of water and chips of ice banged against his teeth. A breeze came in through the window.

The sun wasn't all the way down, a salmon-colored glow lit the sky. Shimura watched the sky as it grew dark and it was growing dark very fast. Now there was just the fading light outside and the movement and colors from the television. He didn't look at the screen, the sky was always more interesting, and he stared out the windows at twilight drinking the last of the water in his glass. He was tired of the blur of the television and he shut it off with the remote control before he got up from the sofa.

He switched on a standing lamp, looked at his own living room as if he hadn't seen it in a long time, turned around and went into the kitchenette. He started opening cabinets looking for something to eat even though he knew perfectly well what he had in the cabinets and refrigerator. He took a package of white and wild rice from a shelf. He turned on one of the electric burners, found a small pot in which to boil water, filled it with hot water from the tap and put it on the burner. He took a handful of salt and dumped it in the water, waited for it to boil.

There was a window above the sink and he stared out of it at the nighttime sky. The sky was sprinkled heavily with stars and there was a quarter moon. Between the stars and the moon his eyes followed an imaginary thread that lead him to Kawamura and Asami, and the thread went on moving until it was attached to Angela and Pohl. But it didn't take him further than the designation of two couples because the thread was beginning to stretch, it got very thin and it was too weak, and then it broke, leaving only the gap between the two pairs since one of the couples made about as much sense to him as a flying pig.

Now there was no connection whatsoever between the couples, the thread disappeared entirely, and what was left was the notion of desire that in one case was solid and real, and in the other wasn't anything at all no matter how hard Pohl tried to make it happen with or without Shimura's help. He thought of what Hadley had told him in the park, then smiled.

He heard the water boiling and snapped his head away from the sky to look at the electric burner and fix his gaze on a point in the kitchenette to take his mind off Angela and Pohl. He poured a handful of rice into the boiling water, turned down the heat. In the refrigerator he found a piece of chicken wrapped in aluminum foil. He separated the breast from the wing and pulled strands of white meat off the bone. He laid out the strands on a clean plate. It would take eleven minutes for the rice to cook.

Shimura went back to the living room and sat down on the sofa. He picked up the newspaper, unfolded it, turned to the page with the rest of the article about the mayor and the corruption charges and the presence of a lawyer he'd worked with on an embezzlement case.

He looked at his wristwatch. When he'd finished reading the article he shook his head. The newspaper really had nothing to tell him that he didn't already know since all there was to know was that everything was constantly in a mess. He let the newspaper down slowly in his lap. He looked again at his wristwatch. Eleven minutes had passed.

42

Fitch stood above Angela in the glaring light of the unshaded bulb. She looked past him at the bulb and couldn't understand why the light wasn't bothering her eyes after she'd been asleep and her eyes had been shut and now her eyes were open for the first time in six hours. She didn't know his real name if in fact the name he'd given her wasn't his own. She didn't want to know it. As long as he did his job he could be whoever he wanted to be. When she'd hired him to kidnap her, he said his name was Fitch.

Fitch looked mildly down at her. His eyes shone. She liked what she saw in his eyes. She liked it when she saw him for the first time just before he'd injected her with a tranquilizer. He gazed past her and his eyes went up the wall and saw the torn wallpaper across the bathroom. She tried to follow his gaze but the ropes kept her from moving enough to see what he was looking at.

She stayed with that other moment, the moment she'd looked up at him from the bench painted green, when she'd seen Fitch standing above her about to give her a shot, and she thought about how she'd had to trust him then and that she really trusted him now because the whole thing, the kidnapping, had gone without a hitch so far, and he'd done exactly what she'd told him to do with the efficiency of a man paid to do a job.

She took it that far and for now she couldn't take it further. From this point on she thought about the bigger thing, the arrangement she'd made with Fitch, from beginning to end, and whether or not it was going to be big enough to change her. She had to find out if it was going to work. The solution seemed far away and right now there was nothing but the light in his eyes.

"What is it you want more than anything else?" Fitch asked, lighting a cigarette.

She shook her head at him. She didn't know what he was talking about.

"I mean, what would make you happy?"

"I like things the way they are," she answered. "But maybe you don't believe it."

"I believe whatever you tell me."

Fitch closed the toilet lid and sat down on it, crossed his legs, went on smoking. Angela struggled a bit with the ropes. She opened her mouth but didn't say anything. He nodded very slowly.

"Too tight?"

"No, not too tight."

"I'm listening," he said.

"A glass of water."

Without getting up, he swung around and turned on the faucet and ran cold water into a glass. He bent down, held it for her while she drank eagerly, and when she was finished drinking he wiped her chin with a handkerchief, then tucked it back into his pocket. He was careful with her because she was paying him a lot of money to do what she told him to do, and he was always fastidious with the things he did when he was being paid to do them.

"I'm still listening," he said gently. He took a drag at the cigarette. "I know you've got something to say that you didn't think you had to say when you first came out of the clouds from the dope I pumped into you."

"I want you to blindfold me," she said.

"What's that going to prove?"

"Just blindfold me, will you?"

"You've already seen us, the guy behind the wheel and me, what's the point?"

"Okay. Here's the point. But here it is because I trust you. Don't ask me why. Just know it and take my word for it. It's important. I want to be sure it's handled right."

Fitch pulled in some smoke and let it out. "I'm listening, for Christ's sake."

"Do you want to know why I'm doing what I'm doing here?"

"No."

"But you'll do what I ask you to do?"

"Yes."

"You're going to blindfold me, and instead of lying on my back looking up at the ceiling with my thoughts floating around up there, I'll be in the dark and they'll float around in here." She nodded her head. "I'll hear what you say, I'll understand the words, I'll talk to you. I'll do it automatically, without having to think of what I'm saying. Just like that."

"I'm no psychoanalyst," Fitch said.

He ran water from the tap, put the cigarette out in it and tossed the butt in the wastebasket under the sink. He looked down at her from his seat on the toilet lid.

"You don't have to be," she said, craning her neck. "Do you trust me?"

Fitch sighed. "A wonderful thing, trust. When you've got it with someone, you've got everything."

"I want to get out of the habit of doing something I've been in the habit of doing for a long time," she said. "I won't tell you all of it because that's not the point to know what I've been doing. But I'll tell you this much, I've been hating myself for it."

"It sounds serious."

"You bet it's serious."

"You've got it bad, whatever it is."

"I don't feel right anymore, something's not working like it ought to be. I've got to sort things out now because it's going to be a lot more difficult doing it later and then maybe I won't be able to do it at all. And you're going to help me. I've given myself everything that's possible to give except the thing I want more than anything else."

"And what's that?"

"I want to be in love."

"Jesus Christ," Fitch said.

The first thing Kawamura did when he got to the agency that morning was to go through the papers on his desk until he found the stack of receipts he was looking for that were held together by a large red plastic paperclip. There was enough money paid out on them for gas and food, film and developing, overtime for Lundquist and Aoyama, and Eto working as an extra man on nighttime surveillance that Kawamura wondered what Shimura was up to and if he wasn't trying to ruin him financially before his wedding. It would come sooner than later and he wanted to save as much money as he could until then.

Kawamura called Asami on the intercom and asked her if Shimura was in the office. He tried to sound businesslike but what came out of his mouth was more a stumbling for words than a sentence. He asked her to tell Shimura to be in his office at five-fifteen. She told him he wasn't in the building but she'd let him know as soon as he came in, and she started to giggle. He got excited when he talked to her. He turned red but she couldn't see him.

He was proud of what he'd accomplished with the agency, he loved Asami, and she loved him. But once they were married she'd have to quit working at the agency and he knew that she wouldn't like that arrangement because she'd already said that it meant a lot to her to earn money. But he didn't approve of his wife working. Not here or anywhere else.

⊣ Rand Hadley wore a jacket, tie and white oxford shirt with button-down collar tucked into neatly pressed trousers. The tie was a burnt-red color to give the sober outfit and his pale complexion a bit of life. It was one o'clock. He stood with his hands folded behind his back rocking forward and backward on his heels as if he were a patrolman walking a beat.

The elevator squeezed out a ding, the doors opened and Shimura appeared behind a couple of women wearing business suits that went past Hadley into the lobby. Hadley stuck his hand out and Shimura shook it, bowed slightly, then smiled at Hadley.

"It's a habit with the boss," he explained. "A bit of respect never hurts anybody."

"I've got plenty of respect for any kind of respect. Where are we going for lunch?"

"A minute, Rand, I've got to make a call."

Shimura excused himself and stepped out of the flow of office workers that were pouring from the elevators into the lobby and out through the doors on their lunch break. Hadley followed him to a quiet corner away from the exit. Shimura stopped at a pay phone, lifted the receiver, dialed, pressed the phone to his ear.

"That's right," he said. "I'll let him know. Yes. Files and bank statements. He'll have it ready. I'll see to it. The usual hour. Okay." He set the phone on the cradle, looked at Hadley and said: "Let's get something to eat."

The parking lot alongside the building was filled with cars, a row of bicycles filled racks placed immediately to the right of the building's entrance, a few motorcycles were parked in an area set aside for them at the front of the parking lot. Shimura waved at the parking lot guard, lit a cigarette, and Hadley waited for him.

They walked a block in silence until they came to a short bridge that crossed the river. Hadley looked around at the downtown streets, the tall buildings that cast shadows along them, the sun shining on the river and the groups of people looking down at the river as it flowed southeast with a police patrol boat quickly skimming along the smooth surface of the water.

"A clean city," he said, waving his hand broadly at everything in front of him. "That's impossible, I know—but as clean as humanity allows."

"You did your share of the work to get us there."

"We all did our best."

"A public servant's got to be made of big stuff—selflessness, determined honesty and decency. That was you, Rand, and you know it. And those qualities were shared by other men and women in the sheriff's department—plenty of good men and women, really. But there were more than a few flawed ones, too."

"You find them in any organization, at any time," Hadley said philosophically. "In every walk of life."

"Nothing and nobody's all bad, is that it?"

"Yes, something like that."

"And the politicos and bureaucrats?"

"That's something else because the Big City boys give off a lot of gas, as usual."

Shimura laughed. "They stink."

"Rotten fish smell better than they do."

The more they talked about the situation the less they liked it. On the other side of the bridge Shimura took Hadley's arm, they turned right on South Franklin Street and went into a restaurant near the Stock Exchange. As it was lunch hour, they had to wait for a table.

When they'd finished eating lunch and were having coffee, Hadley stirred the sugar in his cup and looked closely at Shimura.

"What's worrying you?"

"I've got to give Kawamura an explanation. I've got to tell him something, but I don't want to give up Pohl's private life doing it."

"What kind of an explanation do you owe him?"

"I've spent a lot of his money on a case for a friend who hasn't taken a contract with the agency. Okay, so I'm working for myself on Kawamura's dollar—three operatives, but not me because I'm not going to take a cent while I'm doing it."

"You aren't obligated to say anything about Pohl."

"Kawamura likes to dig at things until he gets to the bottom. Now and then it takes a lot of time. With this, it's a cinch. He'll ask questions, and I don't want to have to lie to him."

"He knows you, that counts for something, doesn't it?"

"It counts for something, sure. I've been with Kawamura a long time. I know how the agency works."

"Then I think you've got an answer, don't you?"

⧧ Shimura was stretched out on the linen sheet thrown over the futon, his hands clasped behind his head, staring at the ceiling of his favorite hideaway, the six-tatami-mat storage room at the end of the hall past offices that were busy in the late afternoon, trying to keep his mind off wanting a cigarette. He listened to the sounds of the agency as operatives rummaged through papers and spoke into voice recorders, finished daily reports and put them in folders, shoved files into cabinets and slammed them shut, shouted down the phone at a client or informer.

He wiggled the sleepy fingers of his hands, crossed one leg over the other, and rocked gently to the left and right on his hips. He exhaled slowly with one leg over the other and heard a popping sound that came from his lower back. He looked at his watch. It was almost five o'clock.

He thought of the conversation he'd had with Hadley at lunch. He'd given Hadley all the truth he could sort out of this situation. Hadley was the best mirror he had and he'd got a good glimpse of himself in the reflection and a better idea of what to say to Kawamura by listening to what Hadley told him. The solution was there if he handled it like a regular case on a standard contract and was as honest as he could be without giving anything away about Pohl.

And it wasn't easy for him with Pohl either. The last time he'd talked to him he'd given him a couple of possible explanations for Angela's disappearance, but none of them satisfied either of them, and so he'd said they would have to wait and hear the story from Angela herself since they were going to pick her up in forty-eight hours. Pohl had sighed heavily. He'd sounded almost unenthusiastic at first but Shimura knew that Pohl was relieved and relief was all that he'd hoped he could give him.

Afternoon light came through the drawn blinds into the room and gave it a soulful atmosphere. Shimura went on staring at the ceiling. He'd feel a lot better when he straightened things out with Kawamura, and then got Angela out of the mess she was in because he'd have kept his promise to find her and hand her over to Pohl, if she'd let him, and then he could go back to his life and the regular contracts of the agency.

Shimura looked at his watch. Asami had told him that Kawamura wanted him in his office at a quarter after five. Forty-five minutes remained before Kawamura came back from his appointment with the catering company for the wedding. Shimura wanted to take advantage of the time to find the right voice for his explanation of the expenses the agency had incurred on the Angela Mason investigation and if that explanation didn't satisfy Kawamura, he was sure he wasn't going to lose his job because of it seeing that what he'd done was what a friend was supposed to do and Kawamura knew it.

He shut his eyes and his mind wandered. There wasn't anything in Kawamura's upcoming marriage that he wanted for himself. He didn't envy anyone. He liked his independence, and from his point of view marriage was a constraint. When he added up everything in his life today, including his girlfriend, Tomiko, he came out better than even, and that was good enough for him.

What he'd seen of humanity from the people who passed through the doors of the Kawamura Agency told him that there was very little to be envied about anybody and that what was behind what looked like a decent setup, either money or a soft-heart routine, was everything human that always involved pain and worry and confusion, and the measure of happiness that came to a person now and then. The setup was a front that protected the truth from getting tossed around out in the open by the wind, what people called privacy, and more often than not, if they'd just admit it, it was a truth that wasn't half-bad no matter what it was.

Shimura got up from the futon and straightened the room and shut the door behind him as he went out. Too much thinking always gave him a headache. He went to his office and took an aspirin, opened a couple of letters on his desk, one from his bank, the other a sheet advertising low rates for a phone network. He tossed the low rates in the wastebasket, swung his chair around and stared out the window at the gradually darkening sky.

⊣ Kawamura was satisfied with the arrangements he'd made with the caterer, and the wedding plans were going forward without a hitch. He was back at the agency, standing next to Asami. He let go of her hand and whispered in her ear, went to his office and shut the door. He used the intercom to tell her to hold his calls. It was ten past five.

Shimura walked down the hall with determination, and as he got to Kawamura's door he turned and nodded at Asami, knocked twice and opened the door without waiting for an answer. It was five-fifteen.

Kawamura stood up, bowed. Shimura bowed, sat down. He faced Kawamura who stared down at him from the other side of the desk. Kawamura held a bunch of papers clipped together. He sat down in his chair and put a worried expression on his face. Shimura held his breath. Through the windows behind Kawamura he saw the elongated clouds in the sky streaked with reddish-yellow.

It started with the worried expression giving way to a look of disappointment and then the disappointment became a plain standard dose of controlled anger. Kawamura had been practicing it like a piece of music.

"Do you have any idea what this is going to cost?"

Kawamura waved the receipts in front of him.

"Who's going to pay for it? You? On your salary? Have you gone crazy?"

Shimura didn't say anything, he looked straight at him.

"Well?"

"I'll pay for it if it doesn't pay for itself," Shimura said calmly.

"And how's it going to pay for itself?" He leaned back in his chair, frowning. "You don't have an answer, do you?"

"It's more complicated than it looks."

"You know that you couldn't have picked a worse time."

"Let me explain."

"The wedding, the honeymoon, and now I'll have to pay for an investigation out of my own pocket. I thought it was over when Violet Archer said she didn't want to go on with it."

"Extenuating circumstances."

"What? No, I don't want to hear it."

"Don't go off half-cocked."

"It's my business, my agency, and I've got plenty to worry about until you convince me there's nothing to worry about."

"Here's how I think it'll work," Shimura said. "I was working for Violet Archer when her investigation pulled somebody in by chance who turned out to be the guy a friend of mine wanted a line on, and so when I got the line on him—and I got it pretty fast—it looked good for my friend, and when the Archer woman told me to drop her investigation, I kept at the second investigation, a lost-and-found job, and when it broke wide open and I found out where she was, it started to look really interesting except that we don't know what makes it tick. But I think we'll know that when we interview her—not today, but soon. Because it's the woman herself that's in the middle of it. And she's got money. And that's where your worries are over. If it's about what I think it's about, and I'm pretty sure I'm right, she'll pay to keep it quiet."

Shimura wasn't going to take any money from Angela Mason, it wasn't the money that interested him, but he had to say something to Kawamura before he figured out for himself what he was going to do.

"And if she doesn't?"

Shimura was puzzled and sat lost in thought.

"Then I'll work for you for nothing until it's paid off," he said at last.

"You won't make a living doing that."

"I don't think I'll have to do it. Anyway, I like gambling," he lied.

Kawamura opened a drawer in his desk, shoved the receipts in and shut the drawer quietly. Shimura got up, bowed. Kawamura half-stood with his hands flat on the desk and bowed his head, eyed Shimura as he turned around and walked out of the office.

Shimura shut the door behind him, walked past Asami and out of the corner of his eye caught her watching him.

44

The Midwestern city's mayor was interviewed for two hours by federal investigators, looking into corruption at City Hall. They asked him questions related to city policies and procedures for hiring, promotion and certain city programs. The sky was still bright with afternoon sunlight when the investigators left City Hall in two sedans with darkened windows.

The hiring scheme allegedly involved sham job interviews and falsified documents and spanned the last twelve years, touching at least four of the largest City Hall departments. Prosecutors charged that the city administration illegally gave out jobs and promotions to reward campaign workers for the mayor and pro-mayoral candidates.

The accusations of rigged personnel decisions followed thirty-two indictments on bribery and other corruption charges in the city's Hired Truck Program. Twenty-three defendants, including twelve city employees, were convicted. The federal corruption probe began with the Hired Truck scandal but has since widened to take in the system of hiring and promotion at City Hall, which prosecutors claimed has been thoroughly tainted by politics and cronyism.

It was alleged that hiring fraud in the administration defied long-standing federal civil court decrees that forbid politics from affecting most City Hall job placement. A defense lawyer suggested that prosecutors were making a crime out of political patronage.

After sixteen years leading city government, the mayor himself refused to say whether he would run for re-election.

"Things like this, you get embarrassed," he said. "Things like this, you get mad. Things like this, you get disappointed, but then you do something about it."

One of the sedans went south on Water Street, near the river, taking one of the prosecutors in the direction of the airport; the other sedan, with a couple of lawyers in the backseat, turned at the corner of Water and Wells Street going east toward the lake and a hotel.

45

Pohl walked up and down in front of the telephone that refused to ring no matter how hard he prayed for it to ring while concentrating solely on a mental picture of Angela until he'd made himself break out in a sweat. He'd lost track of how many days he'd been waiting for Angela to answer just one of the messages he'd left with her service.

He stood in front of the phone, his eyes dull, and he had the helpless look of an animal caught in a trap. He wanted to take a walk somewhere but he was afraid that the minute he left the apartment the phone would ring and he'd be out walking around when he could have been talking to Angela. He was fooling himself. She might as well have been all the way out of his life.

Pohl walked out of the living room and into the bathroom, ran cold water in the sink and cupped his hands under the flow, then drenched his face. It startled him. He unbuttoned his trousers and urinated in the toilet, flushed, washed his hands in hot water and dried them. He didn't dry his face. Not one ritual he'd used had helped him out of his obsession with Angela. His shirt was spotted with water. He went to the bedroom to change his shirt.

He had to leave the apartment even if it twisted his guts into another knot in a long succession of knots that had been tied and untied in his stomach for the past week. The night air was good for him. To be out there in the street with the neon and fluorescent and mercury vapor lights, the people and the cars and buses meant a temporary respite from the overwhelming truth that he was not going to see Angela again.

He'd go out there to relax because there was only so much he could take of the long-term panic that set in when he waited for the phone to ring. He switched off the lights and it was as if a force he didn't know he had in him shoved him out the door.

There were a lot of lights on lower Jackson Street, rich and garish and flooding the darkness with the all-night glow of restaurants and bars and cut-rate shops and throwing off-beat colors in the doorways and on the faces of passersby. Up ahead, where Jackson turned away from him, the colored lights turned away too, and the street made its way down to where there weren't any lights at all, only the bulky shapes of cheap, two-story apartment houses and an occasional dull streetlight and a block-long, three-story parking garage at the corner of Jackson and Whitfield Terrace. Down there it was all sadness and he knew the way by heart and he knew also that he was going to stay right here in the neighborhood where the rich-colored lights kept him company and gave his eyes a fast-dyed break.

The action on the street was blurry in front of his tired eyes, and it was the sort of action that formed a wispy curtain and he couldn't see through it very well and he had the feeling that it wasn't real. He was biting the inside of his mouth. He saw restaurant customers and bar clients and pedestrians doing nothing but walk up and down the sidewalk on both sides of the street. The noise was just noise that he didn't hear at first because he was concentrating on the special kind of night frenzy that had nothing to do with the earnestness of daylight. Then he heard the singular sound of a driver leaning hard on the horn of his car. He saw a couple walk out of the entrance to the Black-and-Tan Bar and into the lurid glow pouring thickly from a neon sign. Pohl told himself that they weren't really there.

He automatically made a move to conceal his face, but he looked up at them through his fingers. He recognized Burnett's face from the photograph Shimura had shown him at the Kawamura Agency. They didn't see him even though the entrance wasn't far away. He didn't know the woman, he couldn't see her face, but she was drunk and having trouble walking, Burnett was holding her up, and he tightened his hold on her to keep her on her feet.

Burnett propped her against the outside wall of the bar, standing just below the neon sign. Her chin was low, almost resting on her chest, and she looked tired and not interested in anything more than taking a break from everything. She was drunk, and she was leaning now against the wall with Burnett keeping her from falling down.

She started to raise her head. Pohl caught his breath. The thought that it might be Angela struck him as impossible.

Pohl stepped sideways very quickly and he was in the shadow of an adjacent doorway. He waited, listening to the sound of his own heartbeat. His mouth was dry. His right hand fidgeted with the fabric of his trousers. His skin itched. Maybe he was wrong, maybe it was Angela, and then maybe he was going crazy.

He wanted a cigarette but he didn't make a move. He wished he had something he could use to smash in Burnett's skull because if it was Angela standing there drunk and depending on him to keep her upright, he was going to kill him. He didn't know if it was Angela, he didn't see her face when they came out of the bar, but in some twisted way he was telling himself he wanted it to be Angela because then he was going to see the contents of Burnett's skull splatter onto the expensive material of his suit with his own eyes.

Let it rest where it is, Pohl thought. You've got nothing to do here but wait until they've gone.

He considered it for a moment, then nodded slowly.

Do yourself a favor. Don't underestimate your lack of brains. If it's her, if it's really Angela, you're going to kill him. But have you thought for a minute about what's going to happen to you after that? No, you aren't thinking, that's the problem. You're making plans without thinking, and you're all too ready to do something without weighing the consequences which are definitely going to take you somewhere you don't want to go. Shimura said he'd take care of it.

Pohl grimaced. His mind kept him on a short leash. He wanted to break Burnett's head, and so he tried to change the channel or switch it off altogether. But his body was just feeling the agitation that went along with his anger.

He inhaled and held his breath. With his eyes open wide he stepped out of the doorway to face Burnett. Pohl had to jump out of the way of a couple that hadn't seen him coming. Then he looked up at the neon sign above the bar entrance, his eyes gave it a good hard look to keep him from having to see what really interested him, and when he couldn't take the delay and waiting his eyes went down and to the right along the wall and kept on going down until they got to the point where the wall met the sidewalk and the empty place where Burnett had been standing with the woman.

He spun around, looked up and down and left and right and didn't see them. He didn't see Burnett. He didn't see the woman. He wanted to shout Angela's name at the crowd moving along the sidewalk. He wanted to smash Burnett's face with his fists. He wanted all of it to be finished. Finally, he wanted a cigarette.

He lit a cigarette, all the time looking at the faces of the people walking past him. He took a slow pull at the cigarette. The smoke seeped from the corners of his mouth. He smiled dimly and thought: There's nothing like tobacco to steady the nerves. He stood there with the cigarette in his hand and all of a sudden he didn't feel anything. He flung the cigarette to the pavement.

Pohl recognized Burnett's suit and the woman staggering alongside the suit on drunken legs, bumping into the man wearing it, skating out toward an oncoming pedestrian and swinging wide and back into the grasp of Burnett's hand. Now it was like Pohl had fallen into a hole and it was not completely black in the hole because a light was shining ahead of him and he thought that if he could just reach that light he'd at last find Angela.

He moved forward quietly and carefully. He told himself to keep it that way even though there was so much noise from the traffic and the chatter of people's conversations and the music that spilled out of a bar, so much noise that nothing could draw attention to him. He gathered his confidence, trying to get in stride again. He followed them, slowly at first, then picking up speed because he was afraid of losing them. They rounded a corner off Jackson, and he was right behind them.

46

Aoyama's legs carried him away from the diner where he'd stopped for a cup of coffee and a piece of pie. He moved along the sidewalk, hopped over a low rosebush and turned the corner. What he'd just read in the newspaper about the mayor didn't make sense to him. How could somebody be so stupid? But nothing made sense to him from the moment he'd entered the house with the woman wearing plum-colored underwear. It was the third day, but not the third day in a row that he'd gone out to bear witness to the excessive behavior of local citizens.

It seemed to him that the whole population of the city had prescribed itself a dose of self-gratification and was busy indulging in a variety of pleasures without any limits. That was all he could make of it because he came to a chain link fence sagging in places with a few of its posts missing that surrounded a backyard of dried-out grass and a messy garden with more weeds than flowers.

Standing on the sidewalk, he leaned forward against the fence with his neck stretched out looking at the rear entrance of a two-story house. The dried-out grass went right up to the first step leading to the ravaged screen door. His eyes went to a table standing on a patch of dry earth surrounded by grass that looked like wispy strands of hair. A fat man came out of the house through the screen door and headed for the table carrying a plate fully loaded with sliced meat. The screen door slammed shut behind him.

The man's legs were short, he wore loose-fitting cotton trousers and a wide, colorful shirt that stuck out over his big belly. His neck was thick and the thickness of it didn't let him move his head easily to the left or right, up or down. He was looking straight ahead now at his destination.

There was a lot of concentration on the fat man's face and it was

the concentration of a clumsy man with a lot at risk, a heavy loss waiting for him if he stumbled and dropped the plate. When he got to his
destination he put the plate of sliced roast beef on the tabletop, turned
and went back into the house through the screen door.

Aoyama heard the clatter of pots and pans, dishes and silverware,
then the fat man switched on music and the music swam out of the
house into the garden. The fat man came out again, this time with a
plate of roast chicken and grilled sausages. His eyes darted from left
to right looking for anything that might trip him up. He made it
safely to the table. Aoyama crossed his ankles, watching him.

The next time he came out it was with a platter of steamed, mixed
vegetables. Latin music played from within the house, following the
fat man into the backyard. Aoyama sighed. The atmosphere was calm
and soft and amiable.

The fat man went back into the house and a minute later came out
with an assortment of sauces and three glass covers for plates and platter. His body moved freely now that the table was successfully laid out
with food and the possibility of losing any of it before he could get his
knife, fork and spoon into his meal was gone. He headed for the table.
His fat jiggled under the wide shirt. He stumbled and almost dropped
what he was carrying when he saw Aoyama watching him from the
other side of the fence with elbows resting between posts and hands
clasped. Aoyama smiled dimly, sort of sadly. Then the smile faded.

The fat man was still on his feet. His mouth spread nervously into
a smile. He put the condiments on the table, covered the dishes, and
walked slowly, as fast as he could walk, to where Aoyama was standing. When he got to the fence he extended his thick arms, and his thick
hands delicately grasped the fence that would have buckled under
the weight of him if he'd leaned on it. Aoyama was not going to take a
chance with the fat man. He moved cautiously away from the fence.
The fat man grinned pleasantly at him.

"It does look good, doesn't it?" the fat man said.

"Well, yes," Aoyama said calmly. "It looks good, and it's a lot of
food, too."

"When you've got an appetite like mine the sky's the limit," he
said with a smile.

He was grinning at Aoyama, but the grin told him not to fool around.

Aoyama couldn't keep the words from coming out of his mouth. "I can see that," he said.

The fat man frowned. "No discussion. Just accept it as a fact."

"Of course," Aoyama said. "I didn't mean anything by it."

"Nobody ever does," the fat man said, "but they say it anyway." His fatty arms hung loose at his sides as he gazed at Aoyama, then squinted questioningly at him.

"It hurts when they say it?"

"Not for long." The fat man winced.

Then he leaned forward and said: "What do you think?"

"Yes, yes, I guess it hurts."

A dog started barking.

"Well?"

"Now look —," he said to the fat man, leaning forward with his hands on the edge of the fence.

The fat man opened his mouth, realized there was nothing to say, and snapped it shut. He was impatient to get to his food while it was hot. Every second or so he glanced at the tabletop covered with plates of chicken and sausages, roast beef and vegetables.

"I've got eating to do," he said at last. "Want to join me?"

Aoyama took a few steps backward and made a running jump over the fence. He landed on his feet. It was hard to focus his eyes, he blinked several times to make the spots go away. He laughed but no sound came out, then saw the fat man pushing two chairs up to the table.

By the time he got to the empty chair the fat man was already sitting down and serving himself from the plate of juicy rare roast beef, spearing a few slices with his fork and setting them gently on his plate. He heaped the plate with vegetables.

Aoyama waited until the fat man was chewing a piece of meat before he said anything.

"How long have you been at it?" he asked, pointing at the plates of food.

"You can tell from the size of me," the fat man said. "A long time, such a long time that I've lost count."

"Why do you do it?"

"It makes me feel good, what do you think? I love food, and it gives me pleasure to eat like a pig."

He gracefully cut another bite from a slice of roast beef, gathered some vegetables, and before he put it all in his mouth he said: "And I sleep good after I eat."

"Well, that's something," Aoyama confirmed. "I don't sleep very well."

The fat man chewed slowly, savoring the taste.

"But your health. Don't you suffer from eating all that food?"

"Don't ask stupid questions."

"I'm sorry," Aoyama murmured. "I shouldn't have put it that way."

"What?"

"I'm bothering you."

"Yes, you're bothering me," the fat man said. "I don't like stupid questions and you're up to your eyes in them. And I don't like being treated like a child."

"I'm not treating you like a child," Aoyama said sincerely. "I'm just curious. I want to know more about something I don't know very much about."

"You're twisting my head into knots with your questions when all I want to do is eat," the fat man explained calmly. "We won't talk about it."

"We aren't talking," Aoyama assured him.

"It's a personal matter and it shouldn't be the topic of discussion."

"That's all right with me."

The fat man plunged his fork into a sausage, cut a piece and put it in his mouth, chewed and swallowed.

"Not up to it?" he asked, his mouth empty.

"What?" Aoyama said.

"An argument." The fat man, smiling, lifted a chicken breast from the plate and put it in front of him next to three-quarters of a sausage, a slice of roast beef, vegetables. He covered the plate of chicken.

"What do you mean, an argument? I'm your guest at the table and I didn't ask you for anything to eat, you offered it, and now you're asking me if I want an argument. I think you're way off. I think there's a problem and I know it isn't just the food." Aoyama frowned. "I won't argue with you."

"Okay. If I want to look back and examine the record, I'll see that wanting to argue is an old habit like all the other old habits, like eating more than my stomach can hold," the fat man said. "But I can't do that, I can't afford to look back. If I do, I'll require another meal right away, a great many meals. And that isn't going to change a thing. So let's put it aside."

"Now I want to try the roast beef and vegetables," Aoyama said politely.

The fat man served him a few slices of roast beef and a helping of steamed vegetables. They ate in silence. The sky wasn't overcast, it was pale blue, the air was pleasantly mild and birdsong punctuated the city sounds that came into the garden.

It wasn't the time to be sitting with a stranger and eating a meal, but Aoyama told himself that he'd have to eat a decent meal sooner or later since he wouldn't get a chance to sit down to eat at the proper time, and here was the opportunity, right in front of him, and he might as well eat now, because the truth was that even though he might be sleepy after a meal he was going to have a lot more energy and concentration for the night. And the fat man was really a very good cook. Then the words were coming out of his mouth again and he couldn't stop himself from saying them.

"I was just wondering why you do it?" he asked.

The fat man stopped chewing and stared at him, pulling a particular face that gave his expression of exasperation a kind of sadness mingled with a pleading to be understood.

"Can't you see what you're doing?" the fat man said. "You're forcing me to talk about things I don't want to talk about. With my mouth full."

Aoyama rested his knife and fork on his plate.

The fat man's eyes narrowed as he went on: "You told me there wouldn't be any talk at all. You've been doing a lot of talking."

"I apologize."

"You might've ruined my meal. But lucky for you, you haven't, my chatty friend."

Aoyama didn't say anything. His head was lowered and he pressed his knuckles against his chin. Then he looked up and let out a sigh.

The fat man's eyes were fixed on Aoyama but his hands went to work on the sausages and a piece of chicken. He pushed the fork into two grilled sausages and then another chicken breast and dropped them ceremoniously on his plate next to the remaining vegetables. He lifted the cover off the plate of roast beef and served himself two juicy slices. The knife and fork were nimble extensions of his fingers. He put a forkful of vegetables and chicken in his mouth.

Aoyama let out another sigh. And then, his voice low, he said: "Do you mind if I get myself a drink?"

The fat man swallowed. "Through the screen door, into the kitchen, on the right, in the fridge. Whatever's in there, you're welcome to it."

"And you?"

"A beer, and an ice-cold glass."

"An ice-cold glass," Aoyama said, smiling.

"Yes."

"In the fridge?"

"In the fridge."

Aoyama got up from the table, walked to the screen door, opened it and went into the house, without letting the door slam shut behind him.

The fat man went on eating, scooping up vegetables and cutting a piece of roast beef and taking a bite of grilled sausage and carving a slice of chicken and pushing it in with everything else. As he chewed and swallowed, the mouthful of food charged into his body with electric-wild voltage. He was high as a kite.

Aoyama came back to the table with a glass of sparkling water, a cold beer, a chilled glass and a bottle opener. He opened the bottle for the fat man, poured beer into the glass leaving a frothy head, put the bottle next to the glass. He stood behind the fat man and watched over his shoulder as he went on eating.

"Thank you," the fat man said without turning around. "You see how it is?"

"Yes, I see how it is." Aoyama said. "I really see how it is." He sat down, put the glass in front of him, started again with his meal.

They ate in silence. The sky was still blue and the temperature of the air was still mild. A slight breeze swayed the branches of trees. There was the pleasant sound of cutlery against the surface of porcelain dishes.

The fat man looked at Aoyama. "You know what I think? No, I guess you don't," he said. "I think you're good."

Aoyama looked up from his plate. "Good?"

The fat man took another mouthful of chicken and vegetables, and after he was done chewing he said: "You always were and you always will be. I can see that as plain as day."

"What does that mean?"

"A man who's not bad," the fat man said.

"And what's that got to do with anything?"

"I don't know," the fat man said, filling his plate with food. "I don't have the least idea except that I know it. Really, a conviction. That's one of the disadvantages."

"Of what?"

"Of saying what you're thinking when you're eating."

"Why?"

"You can't always explain it, that's why."

"I guess not," Aoyama said, finishing his meal.

He kept his eyes on the fat man and didn't say anything more even though he wanted very much to understand what the fat man meant by what he'd said, and yet something told him not to pursue it, not to take it any further because he'd find out more than he really wanted to know.

He picked up the glass of sparkling water and drank from it. He wondered whether or not the words the fat man had used were part of some kind of strategy to get him to talk about himself. The agency had taught him to keep quiet.

"No judgment, just observation," the fat man said. "I guess that's what it is. That's how things ought to be. Anyway, that's what you are—good."

Aoyama eyed him. There was something here that said a lot more was going on with the fat man than the simple fact that he had a big appetite and kept digging into the food on his plate and when it was running low used his knife and fork to fill it up again. But Aoyama couldn't take it beyond that, and whatever he was thinking, whatever his intuition was trying to tell him, it went right out of his mind and into the middle of nowhere.

They were finished eating. Aoyama searched his pockets for a cigarette, offered one to the fat man who refused politely, then lit one for himself.

"Dessert and coffee," the fat man said, pushing his chair away from the table and standing up.

Aoyama nodded, smiling. "That's fine," he said, getting up and reaching for the plates to help him clear the table.

"No, I'll do it."

The fat man stacked the plates on the empty vegetable platter, hooked the tip of his thick index finger into the mouth of the beer bottle and made his way back into the house with everything but the condiments. He came back for the condiments, the napkins, the empty glasses, and before returning to the house he turned around and said: "Maybe you'd like some more water?"

"All right," Aoyama said.

There was a quiet interval lasting five minutes during which Aoyama finished his cigarette before the fat man came back with a steaming Bialetti coffee maker and a trivet, two demitasse cups and saucers, two coffee spoons, and a bowl of raw sugar cubes. He put the coffee maker on the trivet, laid out the demitasse cups in their saucers and the coffee spoons beside them, and winked in a friendly way at Aoyama. He went back into the house.

Waiting for the fat man, Aoyama looked at the things arranged in front of him, picked up the spoon that lay next to his cup and saucer and put it in his mouth and stared at the slanting roofs of houses beyond the chain-link fence surrounding the backyard. His gaze returned to the coffee maker, moved to the right and came to rest on the bowl of sugar. He smiled at the bowl as if it had smiled at him, took the spoon out of his mouth, looked at it, then put it down.

It was a pleasant break in the routine, he thought. It was more than a break, but now he was sleepy, and so he was glad to have the coffee in front of him. He wanted to pour himself a cup but he had to wait for the fat man, and at the same time he was wondering what was taking him such a long time with dessert because he really needed the coffee, he was counting on drinking a few cups of strong, black coffee to get him up out of the chair and on his way to meet Eto.

Aoyama reached into the pocket of his raincoat and found the crumpled pack of cigarettes wedged between parts of his disguise. The pack was almost empty. He decided to wait for another smoke until after dessert.

The fat man appeared with a dessert tray and a pitcher of sparkling water with ice. He walked cautiously, as always paying close attention to where he was going, and he glanced up from time to time at the table. When a single stride separated him from his goal, the fat man looked proudly at Aoyama. He set the tray down, put the glass of water in front of his guest, and then made a sweeping gesture at the dessert.

"Plum and star anise fool," the fat man said. "I made them myself."

"They're wonderful," Aoyama said genuinely.

"You know what a fool is?"

Aoyama grinned but didn't answer him.

"Beat two egg yolks in cream, then fold in puréed plum infused with star anise," the fat man explained. He handed Aoyama a dessert spoon and napkin from the tray.

Aoyama looked at the fat man with a great deal of respect, congratulated him. The fat man accepted the praise. Aoyama lifted the dessert spoon and plunged it into a layer of the fool and tasted it. The fat man sat down.

"That's something, it's really delicious," he told the fat man. "You're a genius in the kitchen."

"It's not the only kind of fool there is," the fat man replied with a businesslike voice. "You can use all sorts of fruit."

Aoyama took another spoonful, and the creamy, refreshing fruit-flavored dessert rolled down his throat.

"That's poetry," he said.

"Now you're exaggerating."

The fat man put the tip of his spoon into the fool and turned it slowly, taking his time, until he had a dollop that he put in his mouth where his alert taste buds evaluated the flavors.

"Maybe you're not," the fat man said.

When they finished, the fat man poured coffee for them, handed Aoyama the sugar bowl. Aoyama put a lump of cane sugar in his cup and stirred it. The fat man put three sugar cubes in his coffee, stirred it and drank it down in a gulp.

47

They were walking quickly now, several blocks away from Jackson, and Pohl followed them when they turned onto Winthrop, a narrow street resembling an alley because of its cobblestones and high walls of apartment buildings on either side. They were close to the river and he could smell the blend of dampness and pollution in the mild night air. The woman's heels clattered against the sidewalk.

It was all very calm on the surface but the undercurrent was an unpleasant rushing of noise on the order of a profound disequilibrium in the thinking process of Pohl's mind. And then his mind was a lens focused on time and he was seeing through a tunnel packed tightly with the urgency of minutes that separated him from this woman who might be Angela, staggering alongside Burnett on Winthrop Street.

Pohl stopped in his tracks. He felt pressure in his chest that had the weight of a bus behind it. It wasn't the pressure of a heart attack but the breaking down of the machine that pushed him forward to follow Burnett and the woman because he was afraid of what he'd find out if he caught up with them and he was afraid of how he'd feel if he didn't. His determination to know whether or not it was Angela drove him on.

The couple slowed down and stopped at the end of Winthrop at the intersection of Winthrop and Front Street, which ran parallel to the river, and it looked as though Burnett was trying to convince the woman not to move, to stay put, and he laid his hands on her shoulders, standing so close to her that she couldn't turn away from him.

There was a single streetlight on the far side of Front throwing light in a wide arc on the concrete footpath above the river and down below it on the surface of water slapping against the embankment. The light didn't quite reach them, they were silhouetted by the glow behind them on the opposite side of the street. And since the light didn't reach them, the light didn't fall anywhere near Pohl, and he knew he was just another part of the darkness at this end of Winthrop and that they couldn't see him.

Burnett's silhouette lit a cigarette and Pohl saw his face, but the woman's face was in profile the brief instant the lighter was lit and he couldn't make out more than the shape of her nose. It might have been Angela. But it didn't make sense to see her drunk. As long as he'd known her she'd never had more to drink than she could handle.

The woman was leaning against the wall near the dark side entrance of a building that overlooked the river. The wall kept her from falling down. Burnett pressed his lower body against her belly, keeping her from moving in any direction. The hand holding the cigarette waved slowly over her head. Pohl watched the glowing end of it move in wide circles in the darkness.

A tugboat or a city fireboat went by with its engine running almost silent on the river flowing perpendicular to Winthrop and a bright light mounted in the forward part of it, very near the upper end of the bow, swept the two opposite sides of land. The beam of light also swept the two figures at the end of Winthrop, and Pohl saw Burnett's hand lifting the hem of the woman's skirt, baring her thigh, and she raised her leg to complement the motion and pressed her knee against him. The spotlight went past them and disappeared to shine on the other side of the river. Pohl blinked and saw nothing but orange-yellow spots before his eyes.

This time he was waiting for the light, concentrating at the place where the light would shine, and when it was shining there he saw Burnett leaning against the woman and gripping her neck with his hand and pushing her head uncomfortably backward against the brick wall of the building.

The light kept moving until it was on its way to the other side of the river, and at the same time that it left them he heard the woman's muffled scream and saw the silhouette of Burnett's hand and the glowing tip of the cigarette and the woman, using her last ounce of strength, shoving the hand holding the cigarette so that it flew away from her face.

But he was already going forward and his legs were moving

quickly and his arms swinging at his sides and his hands clenched into fists and his feet sailing over the cobblestones.

Then he'd knocked Burnett down and was on top of him and he was pummeling his face with his fists until he felt the blood and heard the cracking noise that was the sound of Burnett's nose breaking. The blood he felt on his own skin but couldn't see drove him to throw a roundhouse right hand and it caught Burnett full on the jaw and Pohl felt the jaw give way and then he put another punch into the side of Burnett's face just below the ear.

The boat's spotlight was out of reach of the place where Pohl stood with his legs apart on either side of Burnett who was lying on his back moaning and rocking to and fro and gripping his face with his hands. Pohl wasn't completely awake, and he wasn't really asleep, the feeling was on the order of being a live high-voltage line full of rage, with consciousness and reason gone until the hemoglobin cells got charged with oxygen and increased sharply and reached his brain to relieve the staggering pressure inside his skull.

Now the elementary agony, the dizziness and nausea of anger was gone and he felt the weight of his body and the soles of his feet standing on the damp cobblestones. With an important part of consciousness coming back to him, he looked around for the woman.

She was standing in the same place, with her back against the brick wall and her hands covering her face. She wasn't covering her face because she was scared, she just didn't want to see what was happening, and now that the only sound she heard was Burnett groaning and no punches being thrown and someone breathing hard she moved her hands away from her face and looked at Burnett's assailant, the man who'd helped her.

Pohl didn't recognize her. She was pretty and well-dressed and slim and she'd really had too much to drink. She wasn't Angela. But what he'd just done to Burnett wasn't dependent on whether or not the woman was going to be Angela. It didn't matter one way or another to Pohl because smashing his fist into Burnett was something he'd wanted to do for a long time and it was joined to a real hatred of any torture as a form of violence. It was a great pleasure to smash Burnett's face in.

Now the woman's slanted green eyes were blank and not focused on anything. The sound that came from her was the clicking sound of her chattering teeth. The shivering was driven by something other than the temperature because it wasn't winter and it was mild, and Pohl knew that it wasn't because she was frightened. Maybe it was the alcohol and sugar racing through her blood or the excitement of watching a man beat Burnett up and the hunger for more of it. Pohl took a step forward, moving slowly toward her.

"My name is Violet Archer," she said, trembling with a smile.

Pohl took her gently by the arm.

It was after seven in the evening when Violet left the man with the messy blonde hair in the hotel on upper Jackson Street, and instead of going straight home to shower and change her clothes, she went to the phone booth on East Olive that stood across from Burnett's apartment. She watched the entrance.

At eight-forty a beautiful black woman left the building, walking stiffly and favoring her left leg, and Violet saw Burnett watching the woman from his window as she made her way down the street to the bus stop. As she waited for the bus, Violet saw her rubbing the inside of her right leg through the fabric of her skirt. And the sight of her doing the same thing she herself had done to ease the pain was enough to tell her that this woman had been with Burnett and Burnett had played the game with the cigarette and that she and the black woman shared the same hurt because now they both had a scar between their legs.

Violet was very angry and she was angry on behalf of herself and the young woman standing at the bus stop and any woman who was a victim of Burnett's sadistic play. She wanted to twist a scarf around his neck and pull it tight until he turned blue and his tongue stuck out and he stopped breathing forever. But there was a tingling between her legs that told her she was turned on in a sick sort of way by the pain the other woman was feeling now. She shook her head, lifted the phone from the cradle and pressed Burnett's number. It rang five times and he picked it up.

"I want to come up. Can I come up?" she asked him.

"I'm worn out," Burnett said.

"It'll only be for a couple of minutes."

"Promise?"

"Promise."

Aoyama said goodbye to the fat man and thanked him for the food he'd enjoyed and started to climb over the fence when the fat man took him by the arm and led him around to a gate at the side of the house.

"*I* couldn't do it," the fat man said, pointing at the fence. "And you've just finished a big meal."

"You've got a point."

"So long." The fat man waved a thick hand.

The afternoon was beginning to show in the changing color of the sky. There was still plenty of sun but the way it lit the sky tinted everything with amber. Aoyama felt sleepy but he knew the sleepiness would wear off and the strong coffee and good meal would keep him going until nightfall. The streets were busy with cars that came up close one behind the other and the drivers' impatience gave way to a lot of sounding horns that no one paid attention to.

He arrived at the corner of Barton Road and Hartrey Avenue and turned right on Hartrey and kept on going at a good pace toward the liquor store sandwiched between a market and a Laundromat. In the liquor store he bought a pack of cigarettes and stood just outside the entrance smoking, eyeing the customers entering the market empty-handed and leaving loaded down with groceries. A kid on a skateboard sailed past him, threading his way between the people coming and going.

Aoyama sat down on a bench a few feet away from the bus stop, pulled the photo of Angela Mason out of his jacket again, stared at it, but didn't see her face because his mind was elsewhere, going over the lunch he'd had with the fat man. He dropped his cigarette to the sidewalk, crushed the butt with his heel, put the photo back in his pocket. He was going to meet Eto at eight forty-five.

He left the bench and walked along the sidewalk the length of Hartrey away from Barton Road. When he came to the entrance of the card club called Four Aces, after a brand of Sri Lankan cigarettes, he rang the bell that brought a familiar, skinny little man with a pock-marked face to the door.

"Who is it?" the man asked.

"Aoyama, 301."

"Come on in," the skinny man said. "It's been a long time."

"I haven't been in the mood to lose money lately," Aoyama said, stepping past him into the vestibule. "Or, I really haven't had the money to lose."

"I've heard that one a hundred times," the man said, smiling. "Follow me."

Aoyama walked behind him down the hallway dimly lit by shaded lights from dull sconces evenly spaced along the cheap paneled walls.

The hallway led them to three doors, the door on the left led to a nicely furnished private room, behind the door on the right was the kitchen. The man with the pockmarked face swung open the door in the middle and Aoyama saw the five familiar card tables with five lights hanging down above them from the high ceiling and a lot of cigarette and cigar smoke hovering above the players. Black shades were drawn over the rectangular windows at the opposite side of the room.

He knew a few of the players as regulars and he recognized some of the weathered faces of those he'd seen before but didn't know very well. Some of the regular players looked up at him, but only for an instant. He sat down at a table of four to make it five hands, and the man they called Walter fanned a pack of cards on the table, scooped them up, riffled them as he watched Aoyama put money on the table, turned them over, smacked them down and indicated them for a cut.

Aoyama cut the cards.

"Closed poker," Walter said. "Fifty cents up and a dollar to open."

They'd been playing for more than two hours, and on the next play a man named Parker called Aoyama on what appeared to be a bluff and Aoyama showed him a third ace that beat his three kings. Aoyama told them that he'd had enough and he thanked them and gathered his meager winnings.

He shut the door behind him, stood in the hallway and lit a cigarette, then he heard a scuffle coming from behind the door of the private room. There was a slurred curse, a raised voice and someone shouting and the shout was followed by a loud crash. Aoyama listened to the fight over money that he was used to hearing in the private room of the Four Aces.

He walked slowly down the hallway and when he got to the vestibule he tipped the skinny man who'd got up from the stool near the wall where he'd been reading an evening paper. He opened the door for Aoyama and said goodnight.

He threw his cigarette away standing next to the entrance of the club and looked cautiously up and down the street. At this end of Hartrey there wasn't much going on after seven-forty. A wind had come up but it wasn't very strong. It blew away the paper trash in the gutter and freshened the air.

Aoyama took his time walking to the end of Hartrey, then turned left without looking up at the sign. A few cars cruised along the winding path of the drive. The mild evening embraced him. He was in a neighborhood that he knew very well. He counted his steps and when he got to eighteen he turned right on Delaplaine Road and from here all he had to do was follow this road and it would take him to Lavergne Terrace where he was going to meet Eto.

Five men in worn and filthy clothes stood below a viaduct with disused railroad tracks built over a ravine, warming themselves around a fire that crept past the rim of a rusty barrel three feet high. Traffic ran smoothly along West Samuel Drive, perpendicular to the track, and the five men paid no attention to the sounds of the nightly flow of cars and the human beings in them. One of them bent over to pick up a bottle tucked in an overcoat folded to cradle it from rolling the rest of the way down the ravine.

They passed the bottle around, each taking a judicious swallow after wiping away the saliva where the previous man's lips had sucked at the open end like a baby's bottle of milk. Most of them weren't drunks, they drank just to keep away their cold-death isolation from the rest of the world which no longer thought of them as human beings. The heat from the cheap wine let them feel the blood in their veins. Three out of five men were laid off from work two years ago without hope for a new job, no health insurance, no savings, and it didn't take long before they'd ended up on the street. The fourth man was mentally disturbed and the fifth, permanently on the sauce.

The mental institution was shut down two years ago and the patients were let loose on the city without shelter, follow-up or any direction to follow. The number of employees at the factory where three of the men had worked was drastically reduced after the owners found it more profitable to have their products assembled in another country with ill-paid labor. The drunk liked to drink. The lights from West Samuel at the intersection with the railway tracks threw shadows of a series of arches down on them from the viaduct.

Burnett had made a few phone calls and two visits with a man named Fitch during the period Shimura was having him tailed. Frankie followed Burnett when he'd gone out to meet Fitch on a Wednesday afternoon. Burnett picked him up at the intersection of Paulina and 34th not far from the south branch of the river. They rode in Burnett's car to a restaurant. She wrote everything down, called Shimura from a pay phone, and he sent Eto to the restaurant. Burnett and Fitch sat opposite one another in a booth and drank coffee and talked in whispers except when the waitress refilled their cups and then they talked in normal voices about baseball. Eto sat in a booth with his back to them and heard more than a few words without knowing the context. Later, relying on a very good memory, he put on paper what he'd been able to catch from their whispered conversation.

Frankie photographed them entering the restaurant, sitting in the booth, leaving the restaurant, from behind and beside them at a few red traffic lights. The shape and details of Fitch's ears were clearly visible in four of the photos.

At the second meeting on the following Sunday morning, Burnett's car pulled over to the curb in a drab neighborhood on the Westside and another sedan drove up five minutes later with Fitch in it. Fitch got out, went to the driver's side of Burnett's car and received an envelope from Burnett's hands. Frankie called it in. Shimura identified Fitch from the photos and the shape and details of his ears.

Eto stood out of reach of the glow of a streetlamp with his arms folded across his chest and his shoulder pressed against the supporting wall of a house under renovation on Lavergne Terrace. He'd been watching the streets since seven o'clock when Shimura had given him the go-ahead.

Frankie had followed Fitch from his apartment. He went on various errands in the late afternoon that included a visit to a stationary store and a light meal in a diner, then to this neighborhood where he'd parked his car at Lavergne Terrace. Now Fitch was two blocks away with his notebook and pen in the small, four-room house at 4 Nightingale Lane. Before Frankie went off the job she gave Shimura the information and he'd passed it on to Eto, who'd been working on a divorce case. Eto went directly to Lavergne Terrace. He hadn't been getting much sleep and needed some rest. The total for this tailing and surveillance business came to three days and two nights plus the overtime he was putting in on gathering evidence for the legal dissolution of a marriage that was heading straight for court.

He looked at his wristwatch. It was eight-fifteen. Aoyama had said he'd meet him to get an update on the situation. The neighborhood was quiet, windows were lit by lamps and the light that filtered through drawn shades glowed faintly at the street without really reaching it. Eto chewed gum. There was a cool, soft breeze. He took a deep breath of night air.

Each time Fitch went to Pigsville and the house on Nightingale Lane, he stayed no less than an hour. Eto had marked the time with his watch and kept the dates and times in a file in his head until he found a minute to put them down in a book for Shimura. He did nothing more than wait for Fitch to come and go to the house, he didn't try to look through the windows whose blinds were always drawn, he didn't listen at the door because it was a thick, solid door. But he did see that Fitch carried a hardcover notebook whenever he went in and out of the house.

Eto had been at the Kawamura Agency for three years. Now it was the beginning of his fourth year. He worked with Aoyama directly under Shimura, and Shimura had told him to clock Fitch, nothing more than that, so that was what he'd been doing.

He chewed his gum and began to reconstruct in his mind the last encounter he'd had with his father when his father visited him in a city in the Southwest. They were riding together on a train called the Texas Eagle to a Midwestern city in the region of the Great Lakes.

Eto's father was reading a local newspaper, Eto stared out the window at the scenery. The train slowed on the tracks, coming to a stop. It was the fourth time the train had stopped. Eto frowned. They'd stopped because it was another freight train and freight trains had the right-of-way over passenger trains and this freight train, at least a mile long, moved very slowly with its more than eighty cars trailing behind two engines and all of it curving away from the waiting passenger train into the distance of the plain that spread out toward the horizon.

Eto calculated with his eyes shut that if there were eighty-five cars with 70-foot hoppers and a conservative five feet between them the length of the mixed merchandise freight train was more than 6000 feet long. He opened his eyes and sighed.

When the Texas Eagle lurched forward and the train was on its way northeast again, Eto's father set the newspaper in his lap and looked at his son, and beyond him, the landscape changed from broad, pleasant pastures, grassy flatland and trees to a used car lot and a warehouse at the outskirts of a town. Behind a pair of glasses with thick lenses his enlarged eyes followed Eto's gaze and fell into the passing street of the small Midwestern town as the train went by the offices of the Great Lakes Excavating Company and the cream-colored brick two-story building of Allied Insulation.

"Another small town," he said unimaginatively to his son. "That makes a half-dozen since we left the big city."

Eto turned, looked at his father and smiled faintly.

He started to tell his father to knock it off, small talk wasn't interesting to anybody, especially to him, saw kindness in his father's expression and heard himself say: "The Midwest is the sum of its small towns," with a voice that told of the years he'd lived in America.

A man the size of three men got up from his seat and went past them. He wore a pair of black, knee-length shorts and a black, sleeveless T-shirt and his exposed, large belly hung over the waistband of his shorts. He wore his long hair in a ponytail and had a trimmed Vandyke beard and mustache. His flabby white arms were covered in tattoos. He might've been the biggest man they'd ever seen if they hadn't come from a country of sumo wrestlers.

He was downstairs in the toilet for five minutes. They heard him breathing hard as he climbed the narrow stairs from the lower level of the train car, their eyes followed him when he heaved past using the luggage rack on either side as support on the journey back to his seat.

"A man that size—" Eto's father said.

"Yes," Eto said. "They eat a lot."

They looked at each other.

"Let's get some rest," Eto said, reaching out to put his hand on his father's arm.

"There are blank pages in the book," Eto's father said. "I'd like to fill them in."

"You mean you want to tell me something?"

"I'm not going to be greedy."

"I know that." Eto straightened himself in the seat. "That's why we're going where we're going. The accountant, then straight to the bank."

"I thought it was settled," Eto's father said.

"It will be."

"That accountant hasn't done anything stupid, has he?"

Eto's father gripped the edge of the newspaper in his lap.

"Nothing's wrong," Eto assured him.

"The money I've been sending—"

"We're going to figure it out." Eto squeezed his father's arm. "What you want for yourself and what I want for myself make up a single item we can work on together."

"You want the same thing I want, don't you?"

"That's right."

Eto's father let go of the newspaper and it fell to the floor beneath the seat in front of him. The Texas Eagle kept on its tracks going northeast. Eto bent down and picked up the paper and put it in his father's hands.

"There's nothing to worry about," Eto said. "I want you to meet the accountant. So he can put a face to the transfers you've been sending. He's been asking questions and he's talking about the tax people. I don't want him to get the wrong idea."

"Taxes," Eto's father said, swallowing the word after it'd made a lump in his throat.

Two days later they learned that the accountant, with the help of a woman at the bank, had cooked the books and a certain amount of money got lost and it amounted to a lot of money. A large part of it disappeared without a trace and what was left of it had been diverted to where Eto and his father couldn't touch it and the two crooks could profit by it. In the meantime the accountant had put the government in the picture on taxes due in order to muddy the whole thing, and what money remained for Eto and his father was just enough to pay them. Because the money Eto's father was funneling into the account was itself embezzled from the company he worked for in Japan, they couldn't do anything about it.

His father went back to his job as an accounts manager for an investment firm in the fifty-four-story main tower in Roppongi, a vast office, residential and cultural complex of concrete and steel developed by Mori Building at the center of Tokyo, while Eto, with no money of his own, had to make a living right away, so he stayed in the Midwestern city and went to work at the Kawamura Agency.

Eto yawned, shook his head. He stared at the small garden in the middle of Lavergne Terrace. He looked at his wristwatch. It was eight forty-five. He left the supporting wall and crept to a nearby doorway. The faint glow of a streetlamp lit his face. He heard footsteps coming from the direction of Delaplaine Road. It was Aoyama. They walked silently together along Lavergne Terrace toward Nightingale Lane.

It was a quarter to eight, but the agency wasn't empty. Kawamura was still in his office with the door closed. Asami, just outside his door, switched off the desk lamp and got up and went through the agency and turned off all the lights that other employees left on because they didn't listen to Kawamura when he told them he wanted to save as much money as he could on electricity because there was so much energy wasted in the office that they didn't have any to spare.

The blue evening light and the stray clouds and the end of the working day hung like a veil over the agency, the building, the neighborhood streets and the city. And that veil kept a natural warmth from drifting out of all the inhabitants and the buildings and made the city a particularly comfortable place for the night. Asami went quietly to Kawamura's door and knocked once and went in as if she were floating on air.

Kawamura looked up from the handwritten notes on the yellow notepad in his left hand and broke into a smile. Asami blushed, smiling. There was a long silence and the room was so quiet that the noises from the huge city gradually grew more audible. A car backfired. Kawamura looked down at his scribbling on the yellow sheet of paper.

Finally he observed, as if talking to himself: "If I could just figure an angle to cover Shimura so he doesn't lose face and I don't lose too much money." He looked up again. "Please, sit down."

"I don't want to disturb you."

"You won't ever disturb me."

Asami sat down in the chair opposite him.

"You were angry with him, weren't you?" she said.

"I made him think I was. But I know what it's like to have friends and want to help them."

There was a short pause and taxis hooted in the stillness. Asami had nothing to say to the kindness Kawamura had inside him even though he tried to hide it. She was happy she was going to marry him. The difference in their age didn't matter. Nothing mattered but the fact that she loved him. And she was sure of that.

"Do you want to have dinner with me, Kawamura-*san?*"

He tore the top sheet from the notebook and crumpled it slowly and dropped it in the wastebasket. A large neon sign on the roof of the building opposite blinked on as true night fell soundly on the Midwestern city.

⊣| Shimura edged his car forward in heavy traffic away from downtown. He switched off the music and thought about what Kawamura had said to him and didn't worry too much about it because he'd known him for such a long time and was used to hearing him go on about the costs of running the agency. And Kawamura was soft under the cold surface of a man running a business. But Shimura wanted to make it right for his own sake. He figured he'd be working for months without pay.

Then because he was a human being he started to worry about the money. The worry was more or less along practical lines. He couldn't ask Fitch for money because he wasn't looking for a payoff, in fact he even saw the possibility that he might have to give Fitch something since he'd have to get him to agree to his side of it. He'd have to convince him it was the right thing to do and Fitch wasn't some kid who accepted candy for payment and if he didn't go along with it he might make things difficult for them. A struggle wasn't what they needed to get him to give her up. And what he knew about Fitch didn't give him a lot of confidence in the setup. He'd have to play it as it lay.

Shimura turned right onto Ruby Avenue and parked at the curb. He walked over to the market on 12th. A plump young woman with dingy-blonde hair walked through the narrow aisles gathering items that she held in her arms. Shimura picked out a couple of bottles of sparkling water from the refrigerator. He wanted to ignore her but found himself sneaking a look as she bent down to pick up an item placed on the lower shelf. She wore a jean jacket and beneath it a tight-fitting dress made of some stretchy material that spread out across her round bottom and gave him a good picture of the shape of her buttocks and the space between them.

The man who owned the market gave him a smile and the way Shimura interpreted the smile, what he thought it meant, left him cold. He was just looking at her and didn't want to do anything more than that because it was enough of a pleasure to look at all women. But that quickly changed. He took a chocolate bar from the display in front of the cash register. The plump blonde was standing behind him. He could smell the perfume she wore and it was a good smell and it wasn't cheap. He paid for the water and chocolate bar.

Standing on the sidewalk, he tried to shake off her smell and turn the dizziness he felt into a picture of his girlfriend. The picture didn't develop because Tomiko was out of town for a few days working flights going east and west. He hadn't thought of getting mixed up with another woman, it just came to him when he saw the blonde. He didn't even think about whether or not she might accept an invitation because thinking wasn't what it was about when he was under the influence of a hard-on. He saw his tongue run up and down the space between her buttocks leaving a snail's trail of saliva on fine blonde hairs. He blinked, lit a cigarette, took a drag, tossed it in the street and walked home.

In the kitchen he poured a glass of sparkling water, squeezed lemon in it and added ice. He drank it down and felt the icy cold hit his erection, but that didn't make it go away. The dingy-blonde's buttocks shook before his eyes and his eyes watered as if he were slicing an onion.

He threw off his jacket, unbuttoned his shirt but left it on, went into his bedroom and dropped his trousers. He lay on his back in bed, shut his eyes and masturbated until he came on the back of his hand. He hadn't felt such a strong urge in a long time. He got up, washed his hands, buttoned his shirt, walked around the apartment in his boxer shorts with the shirttail over the elastic waistband and his feet in a pair of lavender socks.

At this point, he wondered what it was about her that had switched him on and made him crazy for sex. He hadn't felt like this in a long time. He wished that Tomiko wasn't out of town. He paced back and forth in the living room with an unlit cigarette between his lips. He wasn't nervous but so intensely focused that he couldn't stop moving. Then he snapped his fingers, lit the cigarette and sat at his desk.

People in the city indulged themselves in anything and everything and the need to gratify their appetites was so concentrated and fine that it seeped into the smallest cracks of the mind and left something like biochemical grains there which sprouted desire and that desire grew until it broke sooner or later through the skin. They did whatever they had to do to get themselves a dose of pleasure. The city had got to him. Knowing this, it was as though someone had moved in and lifted a burning weight from his shoulders.

Shimura put out the cigarette and went to the full-length mirror in the bedroom, stripped off his boxer shorts and socks and shirt. He stared at himself but didn't see anything except his naked body. There were the usual sparse black hairs on his thighs and chest, a patch of pubic hair and his cock was no longer erect. His skin was masculine, muscular and white.

He felt a little weary. He wasn't the man he'd been a few short weeks ago, and he knew it. The search for Angela Mason had made him ask more questions than he'd had answers to, and when those questions were about himself and how he spent his time trying to solve other people's problems without solving any of his own he became morose.

But that reflection lasted a few seconds and he recognized the thinking for what it was which wasn't anything special except a way to make himself feel bad.

He didn't know what he wanted now, but he knew he had to do something to change his mind because standing in front of the mirror looking at himself was making him really crazy. He wasn't going to waste time figuring out what the biochemical grains were up to, he had to get out of there.

He threw his discarded clothes in the hamper and got dressed in clean clothes, picked up money and keys to his car, put on a light-weight coat, turned off the lights and left the apartment.

Standing next to his car on Ruby Street, he hesitated and looked to the left at the corner market. It was still open. He walked slowly toward it.

54

Burnett looked at his wristwatch. It was nine o'clock.

"So, you've got a new girl," Violet said, sitting on the sofa. She narrowed her eyes at him.

He sat down opposite her, covering himself carefully with the hem of the bathrobe because beneath it he was wearing the dark-blue panty briefs Cathy Jones had worn while they were fucking. Just before she'd left he told her to leave them behind.

"What's it to you?" Burnett said, leaning forward to pick up his glass of whisky. The bathrobe parted slightly, he drew it over his knees.

"Drop it. I'm just warning you," Violet said firmly.

"Drop what?" His eyes flickered warily. "What on earth are you talking about?"

"Don't play innocent with me, Lew. I saw her. I saw the way she was walking. Limping, really. You've done it again. You must've done to her what you did to me."

"Now listen, Violet — "

"No, you listen. If you've done any damage to her like you've done to me I'll make sure you're fucked up permanently by somebody who knows how to do the job."

"Don't threaten me, sister."

"You'd better wake up to yourself, Lew." She stood up. "And don't call me sister."

"Sit down, please. You're behaving like a jealous child."

"I'm not jealous because I'm not interested in you. And you know I'm no child. I mean what I'm saying. You're finished with her if you're going to play the kind of games with her you're used to playing."

Violet's arm swung out and knocked the whisky glass out of his hand, his arm flew backward, the glass shattered against a pristine white wall beneath the dark frame of a photograph. Burnett stood up, the bathrobe swung open, Violet saw a pair of women's panties stretched across his erect cock.

She started laughing. She was bent over double and holding her sides and almost choking with laughter. Burnett, smiling at first, laughed along with her until they both had tears in their eyes.

They stopped laughing at the same time. He sat down on the sofa, leaving the bathrobe open. She sat down next to him. Nothing was said for almost a minute.

"Look, I'm finished with you. I don't want anything. No money, nothing. I met somebody and I like him and I think he's for me."

"I'm sure he is."

"I mean it. I don't hold anything against you. Just the scar between my legs. And I'm trying to forget it. Promise me you won't hurt anybody else."

"Okay, I promise you I'll knock it off with the cigarettes." Burnett gave her an insincere smile. His fingers were crossed behind his back.

"What do you say we go out for a drink?"

"How about that place on lower Jackson, the Black-and-Tan Bar?" Burnett said.

"You always did like the cheap places, Lew."

55

Fitch got out of his car with the hardcover notebook in one hand, reached his arm out and put the keys in the lock in the car door, turned the key and heard the lock fall into place and saw the button going down with it, then walked to the back entrance of the house where Angela was tied with rope to the plumbing under the bathroom sink.

It was his eighth session with her. He counted each one of them and put a number at the top of the page before he started setting down everything Angela said in the notebook. She was making progress and he felt at last that he was doing something with his life more than chasing after money and taking kidnapping contracts. He hadn't studied anything like what he was in the process of doing with her. He'd seen movies and read enough books to know that listening was a more important part of a thing like this than asking questions until, at least, he had the right question to ask. Listening was eighty percent, paying attention was essential. It was hard work. That's why he was so tired when he left the house on Nightingale Lane after a session with Angela Mason.

The notebook was already half-filled with words she'd said and thoughts he'd had during each session while Angela was talking to him from her place on the floor. Fitch scribbled in the margins what sorts of facial expressions she made as she told him her story. At moments he felt sorry for her, but he dropped the emotional line for a more scientific approach and listened quietly, directing her thoughts on a path with a few well-placed words.

Whether or not she'd ever fall in love wasn't what his job was really about because his job was to wake her up to a pattern she'd been stuck in for a long time, and that pattern involved a lot of manipulation with her sex.

He admitted to himself that he liked what he was doing and some-times the details she gave him made his cock hard. But there was more to it than that, he'd started to understand something about her that gave him a hint about his own life. She looked very good sprawled out helpless on the floor. He wondered if she'd fall in love with him. He'd read about that possibility.

He unlocked the door at the back entrance, shut and locked it behind him. There was a light on in the hallway, the house was quiet. Then Angela called his name. He left his jacket over the cold radiator in the living room, made his way through the hallway to the bathroom where a low-watt bulb burned in the ceiling. She was upright and leaning with her shoulder against the wall beneath the sink. She looked worn out. There were circles under her sea-blue eyes and the deep color of those eyes was washed out.

"You look tired," Fitch said.

"I didn't sleep, not really."

He sat on the closed toilet seat. "What is it? You worried about something?"

"Give me a cigarette, will you?"

Fitch reached up, moved the blindfold from the towel and pulled the towel off the towel rack, ran cold water on a part of it and wiped Angela's face for her. He went to get his jacket from the living room. When he came back he snapped a cigarette out of the pack, lit it for her and put it between her lips.

Angela took a long pull at it, exhaled, then blinked her eyes, indicating that he ought to take it out of her mouth.

"Thanks," she said. "Can you loosen these ropes? They're cutting into my skin. I moved a lot last night. Trying to sleep."

"Okay."

When the ropes were loosened a bit, Fitch took up his notebook and pen, remembered the cigarette and picked it off the edge of the sink and took a drag, offered it to her, put it between her lips until she'd had a puff, then put it out under the running tap.

"What were you thinking about while you couldn't sleep?"

"You."

56

It was Violet's turn to take Pohl's arm to keep her balance as she walked alongside him a block away from Winthrop and Front Street as they headed back in the direction of Jackson, winding through streets she didn't recognize. She was still drunk from the time she'd spent in the Black-and-Tan Bar, but the confrontation between Pohl and Burnett had sobered her up a little and even though she didn't know where she was going she knew enough to keep quiet and hold on to Pohl's arm.

As they got to the corner of Jackson and Norwood Street, Pohl took her around the corner and straight to a bar on lower Jackson opposite the Black-and-Tan. The doors swung shut behind them. It wasn't very busy. Pohl found an empty booth, pushed Violet in first and then got in on the same side, next to her.

Violet lowered her head, covered her eyes with her hands. She cried without making a sound. Pohl put his arm around her shoulders, her hands fell into her lap, she leaned her head against him. He looked down at her hands. The hem of her tight skirt stretched across her white thighs.

She reached out toward his hand, but Pohl withdrew it before she'd got hold of it. The woman was drunk and vulnerable and Burt Pohl wasn't going to take advantage of it. He was just beginning to calm down after smashing Burnett in the face and enjoying it. He ordered drinks to celebrate. She excused herself to go to the toilet to fix her face. He looked around at the bar.

It was shabbily elegant, a third-rate joint filled with small-timers of all varieties and a few slumming high rollers that came in for the atmosphere. Pohl hadn't been in here before, but he liked what he saw, especially the ruby-red decoration, the lush overstuffed furniture with vinyl-coated fabric made to look like leather and the fake mahogany bar.

His eyes came to a tall man at the bar with a swarthy aquiline face and greasy hair, wearing a tight-fitting dark suit. The man was holding a drink in his left hand and smiling. He was drunk. He leaned over the bar, told the bartender something and the bartender laughed loudly and Pohl saw the tall man's mouthful of teeth as he laughed along with the bartender.

Violet returned from the toilet, Pohl got up, she slid in past him, he sat down next to her. The waiter brought two cocktails to the table.

"To Burnett's broken up face," Pohl said, raising his glass.

"You know his name?" Violet asked, her eyes narrowed.

Pohl didn't know what to say, then he thought of something and tried it on her: "You said it in front of me."

"Oh, that's right."

Pohl took a swallow of his drink and so did Violet Archer. They looked at each other and smiled. Pohl's eyes came to rest on the hem of her skirt. He caught himself eyeing her, looked up and straight ahead.

"I don't even know your name," Violet said.

"Burt," he said. "Burt Pohl."

They shook hands.

Violet picked up her drink, sipped it, looked around at the bar and didn't seem to recognize it.

He wondered if she was still drunk.

"Ever been here before?" she asked.

"First time."

"For me, too. Didn't know it existed."

"You were just across—" Pohl stopped himself.

Her eyes swept the bar, Pohl followed them until his gaze landed alongside hers on the tall man with greasy hair. He was stretching his right leg, he grasped it by the ankle and pulled it up behind him so the heel touched his lower back. He stood there like a stork.

"You know him?" Pohl asked.

"No. Just looks familiar." Violet finished her drink while he wasn't looking at her. "But he's not my type."

He turned toward her. "Burnett's your type?"

"It's more complicated."

"Everything's always more complicated," Pohl said with a frown. "I can tell you stories."

"You don't have to, I've got my own."

"Let's have another drink."

"Right."

Pohl called the waiter over and ordered two more of the same. Violet looked at him now for the first time. She gave him a genuine smile. Pohl pulled gently nervously at his earlobe. She laughed. He blushed. They didn't say anything. The waiter brought the drinks and took away the empty glasses.

They took their first sips in silence. Music came from speakers placed in four corners where the stained walls met the black ceiling. Some customers spoke in whispers, the tall man told the bartender another joke, the front doors swung open and a couple of women came in talking loud.

Pohl shut the noise out of his head, Angela jumped into his thoughts, and he finished his drink with a pained expression on his face.

"What is it?" Violet said.

He offered her a cigarette, put one between his lips, lit both of them. He wanted to talk about Angela and he didn't mind telling the story to anybody who'd listen but a voice with experience told him to keep his mouth shut because Violet wasn't just anybody and he didn't know what was between her and Burnett so it wasn't smart to show his hand just because he was feeling sorry for himself.

He searched for something to say, and when he found it he said: "I don't like beating up anyone."

"Okay, but you helped me out of a spot. I might've let him do it."

"Do what?" Pohl took a swallow of his drink.

"Burn me with a cigarette." She crushed the butt of hers into the ashtray. "He did it once, he'd do it again if I let him."

"What kind of guy would do a thing like that?"

"I told you, I've got a few stories of my own."

"You like it rough, is that it?"

"I wouldn't say yes, and I wouldn't say no. You're too nice a guy to understand. And that's all for the good. But I was with Burnett for another reason, don't ask me what that reason was, and instead, I got burned. No pun intended."

"You mean you're not involved with him anymore?"

"I'm trying to warn him off another woman. Nobody deserves a guy like that."

Pohl thought of asking her if it was Angela that she was trying to protect but he kept the question to himself. Shimura had promised him that she and Burnett weren't seeing each other anymore, but that didn't keep him from wondering what had gone on when Angela was seeing Burnett, worrying about her now and wanting to find her. He wasn't interested in trying to figure out Violet one way or the other.

Violet finished her drink, smiled at Pohl, patted his hand and said: "I've got to be going."

"Okay, Violet. I'm glad I met you."

"Thanks a lot for everything, Burt."

Pohl let her out of the booth, stood watching her as she walked away swinging her hips just enough to draw attention to them.

He liked her all right but he knew enough about her by listening to what she'd said to know that it was because she didn't want anything from him that she was pleasant and honest and flirting with him. In another situation, if he'd had something she wanted, he knew she'd be a first-rate pain in the ass.

57

Aoyama saw Eto in a doorway across the street from the small garden on Lavergne Terrace. He was lit by the long reach of light that came from a streetlamp. Aoyama didn't see a lit cigarette because Eto wasn't smoking, he was chewing gum because he wanted to quit cigarettes, which they both knew wasn't going to last long. Aoyama stopped and lit one for himself. On the soft night breeze that floated toward him, he smelled the flowers and the recently turned topsoil and the fresh full leaves of the lone tree in the center of the garden.

It was a fine night. He wished all nights could be like this but he knew better than to believe in wishes that experience told him didn't come true very often. It was just a dose of plain realism. He sighed, kept on walking toward Eto who'd stepped out of a grimy doorway to greet him.

"What's the latest word on our Fitch?" Aoyama said quietly, as they walked along in the direction of Nightingale Lane.

"The routine," Eto said. "He does the same thing more or less every night. You could set the clock by him."

"Every night?"

"Yeah, and there's a guy that comes around while he's there, wearing cook's clothes, right out of a restaurant kitchen. Nothing but a stack of containers with food in them. I got the scent from where I kept myself out of sight."

"Some kidnappers. Then, we know they're up to something else." Aoyama shook his head. "When you've got money you spend it, I guess. They must be getting plenty out of it."

It wasn't something Eto had to answer so he just made a sound from somewhere in the back of his throat. They slowed down when they got to Nightingale Lane. There were six old-fashioned streetlights that went the length of the lane and an old tree planted between each lamppost whose leaves shone in the light. Eto took Aoyama by the sleeve and they ducked into the shadow of a doorway.

"There it is, number four, and you can see most of the lights are out," Eto said in a whisper. "I guess both Fitch and the cook are gone."

"You didn't see them go?"

"I don't have to see them. I told you, it's clockwork."

Aoyama searched his raincoat for a pocket-sized, monocular telescope. He kept it with him at all times. When he drew his hand out of his pocket, the molded plastic nose fell onto the doorstep. He picked it up, put it back, then shut an eye to use the telescope. "There's a light," he said.

"There's always a light. It isn't exactly luxury, but it isn't the sort of kidnapping we're used to," Eto explained solemnly. "I haven't seen anything like it until now."

"We'll find out what's going on soon enough."

"You talked to Shimura?"

"Yes. It's set for the day after tomorrow, in the afternoon."

"Two days," Eto complained.

58

Pohl turned at Fourteenth Street, went straight to his apartment building, unlocked the entrance door and went in. He climbed the stairs and felt the drinks he'd had with Violet Archer. He was still a little high and he'd been pleasantly surprised at meeting her. There was relief in the fact that the woman with Burnett hadn't turned out to be Angela and the opportunity to smash Burnett in the face had eased his frustration and brought him more clarity of mind than he'd expected from something so basic.

He unlocked the door of his apartment, shut it behind him and locked it. As he made his way through the apartment, he wondered if Shimura would be upset with him for doing some surveillance of his own and he prayed that Burnett wouldn't bring assault charges against him. Pohl went into the kitchen, searched a cabinet beneath the sink for a metal pot to boil water in, sent water from the tap into the pot and put it on the stove.

He went to the bathroom to rinse his face with cold water and shake off some of the fuzziness the cocktails had given him. He wasn't used to drinking as much as he'd been drinking since the night he'd discovered Angela and Burnett together. He dried his face and put the towel on the rack and then it hit him. It was a wave of fatigue that came with the days and nights he'd spent worrying and that wave would've consigned him to the bathroom floor with no chance of getting up if it weren't for the glimmer of satisfaction he got out of the roundhouse that knocked some teeth loose in Burnett's head. It was enough to give him the short-term boost he needed to keep him on his feet looking in the mirror at his tired face instead of being saddled with the feeling he was sliding down a slope. He changed out of his street clothes into his pajamas.

Pohl sat in a chair and sipped from his cup of tea. His head started to ache as the cocktails wore off and he got up to take an aspirin. He liked Violet—who wouldn't like a woman like that?—she attracted him in a cheap sort of way, but he didn't ever want to see her again because he knew if he saw her again she'd bring some sort of disaster with her.

And she'd always make him think of Burnett and the thought of Burnett would drag him down to the picture he kept in his head of Angela with a ball-gag in her mouth and under other circumstances that picture might've made his cock hard if it wasn't that Burnett was a part of it.

The tea settled him down. He called Shimura at home. Shimura told him that there had been a development, that he'd have news in forty-eight hours. Pohl put the receiver in the cradle, sighed. He was excited, but not hopeful, and while he wanted more than anything to see Angela, he felt sick in his stomach because he didn't know what to expect from her when Shimura brought her to the surface.

Pohl got into bed exhausted, shut his eyes right away but couldn't sleep. His mind scratched at the details of what he'd seen a few nights before and how he'd felt since Angela disappeared and even though he came up with almost nothing to hold on to what he did have in front of him was enough to keep him awake for another hour.

59

The owner of the market at Ruby and 12th lived on the second floor of the building next door and he'd known Shimura for years, but he didn't know what Shimura did for a living because nothing personal passed between them, only small talk, and as long as his customers paid their bills the shop owner never asked questions. A voice in his head told him from the start that the best thing to do with a quiet man like Shimura was to keep his mouth buttoned up on private matters. It wasn't just with Shimura that he was discreet, he respected everyone's privacy, especially when it belonged to a client.

Stankovitch was a Slav, and his friends called him Stanky. He was honest, worked hard and earned enough money to provide for himself and his wife and to send his daughter to a local university. He read true-crime books, Slavic-language newspapers and the local city edition, and he took his family to the movies an average of once a week. His cousin looked after the store with him and managed on his own whenever Stankovitch took a day off work.

Now he walked out from behind the counter and went up one of the narrow aisles, down another, up the third and down the fourth, looking at all the products he stocked until he'd made the rounds, admiring what he'd built up by himself with the help of his cousin since he moved to the Midwestern city like other Slavic-speaking people who'd come from a shattered and disappointed country.

The door swung open. Shimura came in followed by a breath of fresh night air, Stankovitch gave him a smile, went behind the counter and stood in front of the cash register with his hands flat on the countertop.

"Well, hello again."

"Hello, Stankovitch. How are you?" Shimura said.

Shimura wasn't secretive but selective about who he'd give his confidence to and he'd never had a reason until now to say anything more than a few words about the weather or the price of an item or to ask after Stankovitch's family. The dingy-blonde had made a big impression on him and the erection that went with it wanted to know more about her.

He looked around as if he were trying to remember what he'd come in there for. The palms of his hands were moist. He rubbed them together, bit his lip hard, then forced a smile to maintain dignity and pride in front of Stankovitch. It wasn't in his nature to ask anyone a question that might reveal something about his personal life just by asking it.

"Stankovitch," he began hesitantly, "I want to know if you can tell me who the young woman is that was in here when I was in here an hour ago."

"Why, yes." Stankovitch cleared his throat. "My daughter, Gracie."

60

Fitch straightened his tie, smoothed the front of his shirt and put on the wrinkled linen jacket he'd draped over the back of the chair. He buttoned the top and middle button of the jacket and looked at himself in the mirror. He looked like a proper therapist except that he'd used gel to slick his hair back and eyeliner to put an accent to his eyes.

Now he had two and a half notebooks filled with the words she'd said and the notes he'd taken and they were held together by a thick rubber band. He took his time finishing a cup of coffee with the notebooks and evening paper in front of him at the small kitchen table tucked in a corner next to the window overlooking the alleyway.

Fitch picked up the half-filled notebook, checked his pocket for his pen, folded the newspaper, got up from the table, and dropped it into a paper sack with the other newspapers he recycled every week. He grabbed a chocolate bar for when he got hungry midway in the session with Angela since he wasn't going to order anything for himself tonight, and he went out to his car.

On Fitch's way to the house on Nightingale Lane a vague uneasiness began to grow on him. He gripped the steering wheel tight as he thought about her unhealthy attachment to him. It was a clear-cut case of transference, he was sure of that, but it didn't make him any more comfortable now that he could put a name on it.

She'd already volunteered a number of sexual favors as she lay tied up on the floor beneath the sink. Last night she'd offered to suck his cock while she knelt in front of him with her hands behind her back. He wasn't in the mood to take her up on the favor.

The fact that she wanted to do it was part of the habit she was trying to break and breaking it was the reason she'd hired him to kidnap her in the first place. He had nothing to gain but momentary pleasure and everything to lose. His job was to work with her on a so-called problem and not enjoy himself at her expense while she went on mixing up sex with love when she wasn't really in love at all. He wanted the money she'd promised him.

Fitch swung the car onto Delaplaine Road, then slowed down as he saw the turning for Lavergne Terrace and a blur of two figures huddled together leaping swiftly out of the beam of the headlights.

It could've been any couple of figures in the shadows lit up by a pair of headlights but something told Fitch that these figures meant trouble and it was the sort of trouble that might wreck his chances of laying hands on the money he was expecting from Angela.

He listened to his intuition and experience. Lavergne Terrace had been practically deserted every night until now. The two figures disappeared without being lit up by a light from an open door, which meant that a door wasn't opened, they didn't go into a house, and if they didn't go into a house he didn't know where they were because they couldn't just disappear unless they were hiding themselves from someone and maybe that someone was him.

Fitch was suspicious. He kept the car going into the turn and left Delaplaine Road behind, cleared Lavergne Terrace by making a right onto a dingy, narrow side-street and drove between grimy brick buildings, avoiding 4 Nightingale Lane all together. He didn't know who they were but if they were watching him he wasn't going to lead them straight to Angela. He'd make his way back to Nightingale Lane on foot from another direction than the one he'd been using up until tonight.

He parked the car under the outstretched branches of a tree around the twenty-four-hundred block of West Balmoral Avenue, a block north of Summerdale, with a big cemetery between him and the lake and he started back on foot in the direction of Nightingale Lane with a chocolate bar in his pocket and the notebook tucked under his arm.

Summerdale was not so quiet as Lavergne Terrace. His eyes pointed downward as he walked along avoiding the gaze of the aimlessly wandering people who lived on the streets, the stragglers and bums and drunks standing in groups, and the individuals sitting on the ground staring at a dismal future or staring at nothing at all.

He didn't like being here with people that reminded him how narrow the margin was between those who had more than something or just enough, and the part of the population that had nothing at all. What really gave him a jolt wasn't the expression on the faces he'd see if he looked up at them, but the fact that he might've been one of them if it wasn't for some luck and hard work that had kept him off the streets. Fitch wasn't born with more than average intelligence and ambition, but he'd kept a healthy fear of ending up in a dead-end street.

Summerdale didn't have any streetlights, the electric bulbs that lit windows in rundown houses made the stragglers look more like ghosts. The moon glowed through sparse clouds, the sky was pitch-black and filled with stars but he couldn't see the stars because they were washed out by the city's lights.

Fitch stopped to light a cigarette and straighten his tie and look around at the street to see if the threatening shadow of a man lurked somewhere behind him using the trunk of a ravaged oak as cover. He thought of the two figures he'd seen and wondered if he wasn't just worrying himself over nothing, but he knew better than that and went with his gut instinct.

Lavergne Terrace came up in front of him like an oasis out of the unwholesome and dangerous street he'd left behind, and he let out a sigh, shoved his hands in his suit jacket pockets wishing he'd brought his gun with him. He kept on in the direction of Nightingale Lane with his eyes scanning every darkened doorway for the two figures. The garden was in front of him, he passed under a streetlamp, looked right and left. He concentrated on the atmosphere of the place. There was something that didn't smell right and he couldn't shake it off.

He'd left the light of the streetlamp and moved into a patch of pitch-black night washed by the faint glow of lamp light when he heard scuffling feet on the sidewalk. Fitch swung around. A stray dog scraped its hind paws on the cement. A newspaper swirled in the air on a breeze.

He tossed his cigarette away, then looked up. Out of the corner of his eye he saw a pair of trouser legs in a doorway opposite him on the other side of the garden. He considered shouting something on the order of: "What kind of a spy do you think you are, satchel foot?"

at the trouser legs, but it wasn't worth the effort and so he just kept on walking with his mouth shut.

Fitch acted like he hadn't seen a thing, started down the sidewalk moving past the garden toward the intersection of Delaplaine and Lavergne Terrace not intending to go to Nightingale Lane now that there was somebody hanging around in a doorway who might've been the police or a detective or just a guy from the neighborhood who didn't want to go home to his wife and kids. Fitch didn't want any witnesses. He decided to take a walk.

The small garden in the center of Lavergne Terrace was behind him as he followed Delaplaine for a short distance, then turned right on Eastview, a one-way street, and sniffed the air which smelled of cigar smoke. He descended Eastview's mildly sloping hill. Streetlights lit both sides of the street and threw light and shadows on the small front yards of dilapidated houses and beat-up cars were parked one after the other facing downhill. He listened for footsteps and didn't hear them.

Fitch decided to cross diagonally to the other side of the street, and he used the move to look left and right before he crossed it. There wasn't anybody following him. He went past a healthy-looking car that didn't resemble any of the other heaps that passed for cars on Eastview. He joined the sidewalk and kept moving at a leisurely pace. A car door opened and slammed shut behind him.

He wasn't going to turn around to see who had got out of the car, but he was pretty sure that whoever it was had climbed out of the recent model parked behind him since he'd got a glimpse of a human shadow in the passenger seat as he went by. He heard footsteps hurrying to catch up with him. He didn't like it. Fitch told himself to keep moving along the sidewalk, told himself not to lose his temper before he knew what it was all about.

The footsteps were very close now, he heard a man's labored breathing, then he felt a hand on his shoulder. He counted silently to three and turned around to face a middle-aged Japanese smoking a cigar, then turned his head at the sound of other footsteps. A similar but younger man came down the opposite side of the street and crossed diagonally, heading toward them. He was smoking a cigarette.

Shimura and Aoyama introduced themselves to Fitch and then invited him to join them in the car for a smoke. Fitch sat with the hardcover notebook on his lap in the back seat with Shimura, Aoyama was at the wheel but had turned around to face them. Shimura's cigar end glowed in the darkness of the car and a streetlight cast a long shadow of the car onto the street. Aoyama took a small softcover notebook out of his jacket pocket.

Fitch didn't grasp the meaning of it right away, but he knew he was in a spot, and it wasn't until Aoyama started reading from his notebook in a voice that sounded almost synthetic that he got an idea of what was going on. Then they showed him photographs. He'd been tailed for many days, every move he'd made was put into words, he'd been photographed going in and out of the run-down house on Nightingale Lane, each move was timed to the minute because he'd been implicated in the kidnapping of Angela Mason.

Fitch tossed his cigarette out the open window. It was nothing but the truth and there wasn't a thing for him to say and now he waited for Shimura to put him in the picture. Aoyama closed his notebook and put it back in his pocket, lit another cigarette. A car turned the corner onto Eastview and its headlights swept the parked car with the three of them sitting in it.

Shimura started out slow, explaining to Fitch that they represented no one but themselves, not even the agency they worked for, they didn't want money, they just wanted to straighten out a problem, and he told Fitch what he wanted him to do and how it was going to be done. There might even be something in it for him. And there wasn't going to be any trouble for Angela, what they were going to do was in her best interest, in everyone's best interests, and it'd pay to do what he told him to do because there was always the police.

Fitch shook his head, frowning.

"You agree it's the right thing to do?" Shimura said, smoking his cigar.

"It's not what you think it is," Fitch protested. "I haven't kidnapped her, not really."

"Then what do you call it?" Aoyama demanded.

"I can't talk about it." Fitch looked past Aoyama's face through the windshield at the lampposts.

"All we're doing here is having a little discussion, but the police will call it kidnapping," Shimura said. "Why don't you just let her go?"

"She can go any time she wants to," Fitch said.

"Then how about right now?" Aoyama said.

"It's more complicated than that."

"All you've got to do is let her go," Shimura said.

"She trusts me now."

"There'll be money in it for you," Aoyama reminded him.

"And it's because she trusts you that it's going to be okay," Shimura said.

"I don't like breaking up that sort of thing," Fitch said.

He chose his words carefully, they were informal and solemn because he was defending himself even though he didn't like having to defend himself, but they'd put him neatly in a corner and now he was having a bout with his conscience.

"What sort of thing?" Aoyama said.

"Trust."

"Be practical."

"Of course, trust. I understand that," Shimura said. "I wouldn't betray someone's trust either."

"Then you've got my point. I'm spending considerable time with her, listening. I want to help her, now it's important to me. She asked me to—"

"You don't have to explain yourself," Shimura interrupted him. "Just hear what we've got to say. You abducted her."

"But—"

"If she has confidence in you, then all you've got to do is convince her that it's the right thing to do to let her go," Aoyama reasoned.

"Therapy," Fitch said.

"What?"

"What she's asked me to do for her, it's a sort of therapy."

He'd betrayed Angela with a singular confidence and now Fitch felt sick and he asked Aoyama for another cigarette because he didn't want to reach abruptly into his own pocket and then he sat there smoking it without moving his eyes from the quiet street beyond the window. No one said a word.

"Then she's got to go home, to give herself up if that's what it's about, and to keep it out of the papers—she'll have to pay *you* for that," Aoyama said at last. "She'll be glad to pay whatever you ask." He paused. "Maybe there'll even be some left over for the agency." He looked at Shimura, who wasn't looking at him.

Fitch turned his head sharply around to stare at Aoyama, his face contorted with anger, then he faced Shimura.

"As far as we're concerned, we don't want anything but her safe return," Shimura said calmly, trying to reassure him.

"I'll take the salary she's offered me, nothing more. And you won't get anything out of it," Fitch said. "At this stage of the treatment, I can't stop. I won't change a thing."

"Okay, Fitch, suit yourself." Aoyama flicked his cigarette out the window and gave Fitch a threatening look.

"What are you going to do about it?" Fitch asked firmly.

"What do you think we're going to do?"

"Hold on a minute," Shimura said to Aoyama, playing his role as they'd arranged it. "It's better to reason with him than to have to turn him over to the police."

"Maybe it is, but he isn't doing us any favors."

"Why should I?"

"What do you suggest?" Shimura said.

"I'll let you know. But right now I've got to get over to 4 Nightingale Lane," Fitch said, reaching for the door handle.

"Wait a minute," Shimura said.

"I'm late," Fitch said, letting go the door handle, turning toward Shimura. "She won't know what time it is because she doesn't have a watch, but she'll know that I'm late and it'll work against what's taken a week to accomplish."

"You're a responsible man, Fitch." Aoyama faced the windshield and the night beyond it.

Fitch ignored him, reached again for the handle. As he got out of the car Shimura gave him a card with a phone number on it. Fitch turned around, stuck his head through the open window and said: "It may take a bit of time but we'll do our best."

"Hurry it up, Fitch. We'll give you twenty-four hours," Aoyama said.

The two men in the car wore satisfied expressions on their faces as they watched Fitch walk away, then looked at each other and smiled because what they knew about Fitch was that he was one of the few men in that line of work who played it straight.

Violet rubbed the sleep from her eyes. It was a late morning for her, already midday, and she'd just got out of bed. She stared at the clock on the wall next to the refrigerator. It was twelve-thirty. She made herself a cup of coffee, then sat at the kitchen table and stared out the window at the trees in the adjacent yard, a red pine and two eastern red cedar trees with sturdy branches.

She was already finished with the man who'd been at the hotel bar on Jackson. She'd gained nothing from it but another layer of disappointment in herself because it had ended badly just as nearly all her relationships with men came to a bad end. His messy blond hair and soft gray eyes were out of her life as quickly as they'd entered it. She hadn't been as careful with him as she should have been and he turned out to be a lot smarter than she thought he was.

But she never felt better than when she found herself in a jam since a good thing in the shape of a new idea always came to her out of a difficult situation. She worked best when she was in a corner and had to fight her way out of it and the pressure was too much and it squeezed her thoughts hard until they forced a spark in her head that gave her a new idea.

She was still short on cash or at least she always thought she was and she wanted to get her hands on some money so she figured she'd catch somebody else sleeping who wasn't expecting anything more than the routine and she'd make them pay for walking in their sleep.

The first cup of black coffee went down smoothly and she accompanied the second with two slices of toasted bread and strawberry and rhubarb conserve and when she'd finished the second cup her mean, scheming little mind thought of the man who'd smashed in Burnett's face, Burt Pohl.

Angela leaned awkwardly against the filthy bathtub with her hands tied behind her back and her eyes blindfolded as Fitch sat quietly reading the notes he'd taken from their last session. He wasn't bothered by what Shimura and Aoyama had said and he didn't want to waste any time worrying about it until he'd pulled Angela a bit further along the path she'd made for herself by speaking the truth.

He looked at his wristwatch. It was nine-thirty. He straightened his tie and smoothed it down under his crumpled linen suit jacket.

"I want to see your face," she said.

He put the notebook on the edge of the sink and untied her blindfold.

He ignored her steady gaze, picked up his notebook and said: "Let's begin." He caressed the barrel of the pen with his fingertips, waiting.

"You're late." Her voice was quiet.

He didn't reply. She looked at him without blinking her sea-blue eyes.

"I was worried you wouldn't come."

He calmly returned her gaze.

"I know that I love you," Angela said. It came out of her mouth like a shot.

Fitch didn't say a thing.

She repeated: "I love you, you know." Her voice trailed off.

He cleared his throat and said at last: "Here's what I'm going to do. I'm going to let it ride. I'm going to sit back and watch you louse yourself up. And come to think of it, it'll be a pleasure."

"That's a terrible thing to say to anybody."

"I'm trying to make a point," he said.

"You don't believe me." She'd made a flat statement that struck him as the truth.

"That's more like it," he said, nodding. "No, I don't believe you. I know that you believe what you're saying, but it's not love."

"No, Fitch. I'm leveling with you."

"You've been playing with that thought since the other night when it came to you."

"What are you talking about?"

"I mean the love angle."

"Angles have got nothing to do with it," she said, her voice turning a bit aggressive. "I'm being straight with you and you know it."

Fitch scribbled a line in his notebook.

"Quit writing and listen to me."

He looked up but kept a cool and self-confident expression on his face. "Go on," he said professionally.

"Have a heart," she pleaded. "Don't you feel anything like love for me?"

It was his turn to get upset because he didn't like being on the wrong end of an interrogation which is exactly how he felt now that she'd asked him this question. Instead of arguing with her, he shut the notebook, lit a cigarette and took a long stiff drag at it and took his time letting the smoke out.

"Okay, you don't want to talk about it. Maybe not now, but later. I can wait," she said.

Fitch watched her try to find a comfortable position. He finished the cigarette, put it out under the running faucet, turned off the faucet, tossed the butt into the wastebasket and picked up the notebook but didn't open it.

"This deal tonight isn't something new for you," he said. "For years and years you've been dragging yourself down into a kind of swamp thinking you're in love or just fucking somebody because it took your mind off what you really wanted which was something you thought you couldn't have and didn't deserve and it was too painful knowing it, and believing it was true, so you kept on with what you've been doing all your adult life. And now you think you love me because I'm listening to everything you say without making a judgment, that love's the answer when it isn't the answer because when the answer comes it won't come from the outside or somebody else."

"How am I supposed to know when it's really love?"

"You aren't listening," he said impatiently, tapping the pen on his knee.

"I'm trying to figure it out."

"I'm no therapist."

"Go on."

"For you, here with me, it's a shift of the emotions you had when you were a kid, the transfer of feelings about a parent to an analyst, me, and it happens in all kinds of nickel and dime therapies and maybe in a way between so-called normal couples or even close friends, but it isn't love. And because that isn't love, this isn't love. Do you follow me?"

"So, what do you suggest?"

"You won't know love until it's really love."

"That's a load of shit!"

"Call it what you like," Fitch said, opening the notebook. "I don't give a damn whether you buy it or not. It's just the way I see it."

He was trying every possible way of manipulating her present state of mind to the point of making her more frustrated in the hope that she'd find her own way out of it. As far as Fitch was concerned therapists were crazy. Finally, he'd be glad to get out of it himself and he saw the advantage of having got caught by Shimura. Still there was more work to do and he thought of the twenty-four hours Aoyama had given him.

"Put the blindfold back on and leave me alone," Angela said.

"We aren't finished yet."

"We are as far as I'm concerned."

Fitch was trying not to look at her. But Angela's sea-blue eyes were doing something now, operating like tiny fishhooks, and Fitch went on trying to turn his head and couldn't turn his head. He sat there staring, waiting.

Angela was looking up at him, and she looked at him for a moment that had depth and weight, as if it were something she held in her hand.

He heard Angela saying: "Maybe you're right, maybe there still are a lot of things to talk about and you were just trying to give me a healthy push in the right direction because my mind needs clearing and that's what I've asked you to do for me and it's why we're here. Is that it?"

"Now that sounds like a load of shit."

"Answer me."

He didn't want to explain anything to her, it wasn't part of the setup, but he heard himself saying: "Yes, okay. Something like that."

"I figured as much." Angela smiled at him, content with herself.

Fitch excused himself for a minute, got up and went to the kitchen for a bottle of cold water from a small refrigerator he'd installed beneath the kitchen sink. He picked up a spare glass from the counter-top.

Back in the bathroom, he poured out two glasses, held one to her lips, then set it on the floor beside her. He swallowed a couple of mouthfuls from his glass of water, sat down on the lowered toilet seat and took up his pen and notebook.

"Let's begin," he said.

She started talking, looking at the floor, ceiling and walls.

He thought of the arrangement they'd made and the money that was part of it although it counted less to him now than at the start, and he figured he might have to extend the twenty-four hours he was given by Aoyama because she had more progress to make and it would take as much time as it took for her to get where she had to go by the time the sessions came to an end.

[64]

Shimura was surprised when he'd learned that the plump young girl named Gracie was in fact Stanky's daughter and that he'd wanted to fuck her and couldn't get the picture out of his mind of her spread buttocks, and he didn't feel any shame because of it. It wasn't written on his face so Stanky could see it, and so he figured that what really bothered him was the lack of guilt he felt and how it made him close to and hardly different from the inhabitants of the city chasing pleasure without a conscience.

He scratched his chin, thinking. He was turning out to be just like them. He'd fought with himself and lost on the subject of fidelity while his girlfriend flew east and west, and even though he hadn't followed through with it infidelity jumped around in his head like a nervous rat.

He unlocked the door of his apartment, went in. His mind was a bit foggy. He felt the unusually potent stimulation he'd got from looking at Gracie, but didn't want to get rid of the feeling by masturbating a second time. This personal question of self-gratification was something he'd have to figure out without talking to Rand Hadley. The bigger question of how the same subject affected the city was something else. It was late enough to get into bed and read a book but that didn't interest him either and so he went to the kitchen to make himself a cup of tea.

The phone rang as he poured boiling water into a cup with a teabag dangling in it. He picked up the receiver with one hand while he raised and lowered the teabag with the other. It was Tomiko calling him from the hotel flight attendants stayed in on their layover, and Shimura was immediately drawn away from the obsession with Gracie and his hard cock moved logically toward Tomiko even though she was far away.

Maybe there was something they could do about it since the phone was made for conversation and conversation could be whatever two people wanted to talk about and right now he wanted more than anything to talk about sex and it wasn't the first time they'd done it over the phone on account of her traveling. Shimura's mouth formed itself into a big grin that seemed to come from way back in his throat and it was made of pure satisfaction.

Violet found the bar without much trouble, remembering it was opposite the place she'd gone to with Burnett before he'd tried to burn her with a cigarette for a second time at the intersection of Winthrop and Front Street. She remembered it even though she'd had a lot to drink that night, first with him, then with Pohl after he'd settled her account with Burnett by beating him up.

She wanted Pohl to be there so that she could size him up under better circumstances than the first night she'd met him because tonight she hadn't swallowed a drop of vodka.

She made her usual entrance with her narrow hips swinging just enough to draw attention from the customers who had the habit of watching the door open and close as drinkers came and went. The hem of her lightweight charcoal-gray skirt was well above her knees and she wore a matching jacket over a deep-blue silk shirt. The heels she wore accentuated her bare legs and the muscles of her calves.

Violet's eyes searched the room for Pohl and didn't find him. The hands of the clock behind the bar said ten o'clock. The bartender nodded at her just like every bartender in every bar acknowledged her as she sat on a stool in front of him. She ordered a lemon vodka and ice, which she intended to drink slowly.

The bartender served her a straight vodka with a squeeze of lemon over a few ice cubes since that was all he had behind the bar, there weren't any imported bottles back there except whisky. She spun the ice cubes around the inside of the glass with a red plastic stirring stick that had a ball at the end of it. She turned the stick around and submerged the ball, twirling the stick between her fingers, then drew it out and stuck it in her mouth, tasting the sting of cheap liquor on her tongue. She took a mouthful, swallowed it.

When the stuff reached her stomach she had to catch her breath because it burned like fire as it went down and she could almost hear it hissing as it tore her throat up on its way down to her belly.

She tilted her head back, her hair cascaded like a baby waterfall over her shoulders and for a second she didn't ever want to have another glass of vodka for the rest of her life if they were all going to taste like this. She snapped her watery eyes shut until she got used to the taste in her mouth. Now she understood why Pohl had ordered cocktails for them because a cocktail covered up the taste of cheap liquor.

She shifted her position on the bar stool when she saw her skirt had gone far up her bare thighs showing the customers more than she thought was a good idea since she was alone in a third-rate joint without a man to keep her company.

She took another swallow of vodka, a small one this time, and thought of Pohl as financial support, and then she wondered why he'd taken her to a dive like this if he had any money because if he did he wouldn't bring a respectable woman to a third-rate bar unless he didn't want to spend anything in which case it wasn't going to be easy to play him for big stakes.

She took a cigarette out and the bartender lit it for her and she looked around the room. There wasn't anyone in the bar who hadn't noticed her slanting eyes and jet-black hair. She finished her drink and ordered another. With each swallow of vodka she grew more confident and didn't mind if she gave them all a good view of the fine soft hairs on her thighs. She wasn't thinking about Pohl anymore. No one came up to talk to her even though she felt the atmosphere was charged with sex and that she was the source of it.

A couple of customers left the bar but were replaced right away by a young man and woman who came in together out of the warm night, seemed to know everyone and must have been regulars. Then Violet remembered she had come here to find Pohl. She waved at the bartender and he came over to her and leaned on the bar to get as close as he could to the face with a pair of green cat's eyes.

"What can I do for you?"

"You can answer a question for me."

"Ask it, anything."

"Don't get funny."

"What's funny? I'm just looking."

"You get any closer you'll be in my drink."

"That's not where I'd like to be."

"And I'd rather be someplace else."

"I can look, can't I?"

"Just don't burn yourself up doing it."

He pulled his face away from her. "Okay, what do you want?"

Violet described Burt Pohl using what she remembered of him from the night they were together in the bar to give the bartender an idea of what he looked like and she gave him just enough of a picture so he could help her out on how often Pohl came into the place.

"Yeah, he comes in here, but he isn't a regular—if that's what you want to know."

"That's what I wanted to know."

"I don't even know his name."

"And you won't get mine, either."

"Did I ask you for it?"

"Pour me another vodka, will you?"

The bartender turned around and fixed another lemon vodka for Violet. He put it down in front of her and picked up the empty glass, eyeing her.

Time passed slowly, she drank heavily waiting for Pohl. She swung around on the bar stool. She looked around the room watching the customers until she got tired of seeing the same faces and the faces were men looking at her and trying to catch a glimpse of what she had under her skirt.

Now when the door opened and closed, she didn't pay attention to it. Somehow she'd get Pohl's phone number and call him tomorrow night. There was nothing to keep her busy but cheap liquor and cigarettes and dreaming with vodka-soaked eyes wide open.

66

Shimura's car was parked at the end of Nightingale Lane away from where it intersected Lavergne Terrace, and he sat behind the wheel tapping his fingers on it waiting for Fitch who'd said that he'd meet him here at nine. He watched the road behind him through the rearview mirror. He looked at his wristwatch. Aoyama and Eto were a block away in a car belonging to the agency.

At five past nine Shimura saw Fitch coming up the lane toward his car. He leaned across the passenger seat, raised the handle and opened the door for him. Fitch got in and shut the door, lit a cigarette.

"Is she ready to leave Pigsville?" Shimura asked.

"Everybody's ready to leave Pigsville."

Then Fitch explained the setup within the limits of what he called a professional secret since he wasn't going to say anything private that had passed between them, and Shimura said that he didn't want to know more about Angela than what he had to know if it didn't have anything to do with why she'd disappeared and the fact that she'd arranged it all herself.

"It's got plenty to do with why she disappeared but it isn't any of your business," Fitch said.

"Okay, we agreed that you wouldn't say anything about what you haven't got the right to talk about," Shimura said. "I'm just a little curious."

"That's right. And the answer is no, she's not ready."

"What does that mean?"

"I want to see her tonight, then we can do it. I'll bring her out tomorrow."

"When?"

"In the afternoon."

"Have you figured out your end?"

"That's none of your business either." He paused, then added: "And you better not have any plans of your own."

Shimura looked at him, squinting, and shook his head.

"Right." Fitch opened the door and tossed his cigarette out into the lane. He got out of the car.

"Fitch, there's always the police. You didn't forget that?"

"It works both ways. Quit threatening me."

67

It was almost closing time, the clock on the wall behind the bar said one forty-five. The bar wasn't empty, the customers were finishing their drinks, and Violet, sitting awkwardly on a bar stool, tipped back her glass of vodka and swallowed what was left of it and the ice cubes banged against her front teeth.

The bartender watched her as he cleaned and dried glasses, wiped down the bar and organized the bottles in neat rows one behind the other. She sat self-consciously straight on the bar stool and her eyes opened and closed regularly without staying shut more than a couple of seconds. Her charcoal-gray jacket hung from the back of the stool, her deep-blue shirt was unbuttoned at the neck and when she leaned forward he saw her breasts. Her shiny knees seemed to wink at him each time she swung around on the bar stool as he went past her going to and from the cash register.

Violet didn't hear anything from behind the curtain of vodka because there was no sound where she was, there was nothing but thick quiet, and she saw the bartender moving around behind the bar with his feet not touching the floor picking things up and setting them down and wiping the cheap imitation mahogany bar with a rag.

The bartender had his back to Violet for some moments, then he shut the cash register drawer and turned to look at her, and while he was looking he took a few steps until he was standing across the bar from her.

He said: "Since the other night I've been carrying a lot of weight. In here." He tapped his chest with a couple of fingers but kept on looking into her bleary green eyes. "I remember you, and I remember the guy that was with you." He leaned forward against the bar. "Tonight that weight got too heavy for me to carry. I got to find a way to get rid of it. I'm in love with you." He kept a straight face when he said it, but she couldn't make out any part of his expression.

Violet was focused on a point above the bartender's eyes because the eyes themselves were dancing from left to right and right to left in front of her and she couldn't catch them long enough to look him straight in the face. His voice floated out of some faraway room and into her head and she heard the words but couldn't figure out what they meant.

The bartender stood up straight and now her eyes connected with his eyes and she saw a sparkling light in them that hadn't been there earlier and the light drew her in and kept drawing her in and suddenly it didn't matter what his words were telling her because the glow in his eyes said everything. The light seemed to move around in a slow circle and the circle held her and she couldn't move.

Words gathered in her mind and formed at the back of her throat and came out of her mouth slurred: "You got any money?"

"What?"

"Are you rich?"

"You're drunk."

"Maybe I am. But it's a question."

"I'm not asking you if you're drunk. I'm telling you."

"You don't have to tell me, I know I'm drunk."

"You want to know if I'm rich?"

"That's right."

"Fuck you."

"I'm considering it, but you've got to tell me if you've got money."

The sparkling light in his eyes went out and the circle that kept her from moving let her go suddenly and she slipped off the bar stool and landed on the floor among crushed cigarette butts with her skirt twisted up around her waist.

"There's no happily-ever-after, it doesn't exist, and it's ridiculous to think it might exist because you'd be encouraging a completely crazy thought to become reality and there's no chance of that happening. None," Fitch said.

He shut the notebook, put the pen in his pocket, took out a hand-kerchief and wiped his mouth after he said this and hoped that by saying it he didn't leave any room for her to keep on imagining that she loved him and he loved her and they'd spend their lives together doing what people did when they believed in something as close to a lie as this complete, undiluted bullshit. Fitch was exhausted.

"I don't love you," he added.

Angela stared at him from her tied-up position on the bathroom floor. The bare bulb gave her pale complexion a yellow hue.

"You've got to get it right in your head," Fitch said.

"You're breaking my heart," she said quietly. "I'm in love with you."

Angela meant what she said, he saw that much in her eyes and heard it in her voice, but he wasn't going to give up trying to get through to her before he let her go. It was a promise he'd made to himself and he wasn't going to back down on it. But he felt the pressure of the quiet as she looked sadly at him, as though the lack of sound were something heavier than any sound.

"I've been doing my job too well," he said. "Don't you see that? It's a clinical thing."

"I don't see anything. I know that what I'm saying is right."

"I'm trying to help you."

And then the quiet was heavier.

"I can't do it alone."

She went on staring up at him from the floor without saying a word, and then a very small voice said: "Count me out."

Shimura pulled his car alongside the agency car standing in the shadows on Delaplaine Road with its headlights out and its motor running and Aoyama behind the wheel with Eto sitting next to him in the passenger seat while together they were smoking cigarettes and listening to the radio and watching his car glide toward them and come to a halt in the night.

"It's fixed," Shimura said to Aoyama through the open window. "For tomorrow afternoon."

Aoyama turned toward Eto, asked him if he'd heard Shimura. Eto nodded his head and tossed the end of the cigarette out in the street.

"Go get some sleep," Shimura said.

The agency car drove away with its headlights on and turned left at Hartrey Avenue, and as he watched the taillights go around the corner he thought of Tomiko who was waiting for him at his apartment because her flight had come in at eight and now it was nearly ten o'clock.

Lying in bed next to Tomiko was the single most important thing Shimura had in mind as he swung the car around and headed towards Hartrey and turned right and kept on going without seeing much of the road except what was absolutely necessary to see so he didn't get into an accident because an accident would slow him down and he didn't want anything to stop him now. He was waiting to press his mouth between Tomiko's legs, taste her, and feel her lips against his own when they kissed.

Pohl sat in a chair at his desk in front of the phone waiting for it to ring. It seemed to him that it was the only thing he'd been doing for days and that the rest of his life would be spent waiting for one thing or another. Shimura had told him he'd call at eleven to let him know what he'd learned from Fitch, whose name he didn't use since it was against the rules Shimura'd made for himself, and so he referred to him instead as just another source of information.

Pohl felt the terrible slowness of passing time. It was only ten-fifteen. It seemed like he was bolted to the chair, and then suddenly, somehow he was a long way off from the grief and everything because he was working to keep his thoughts as far from the telephone as he could by stretching them like rubber bands until they were taut and thin and might snap. It was a risk, and he knew that once they snapped he'd come back to where he was, which wasn't a comfortable place to be.

So then he was wondering what he ought to be thinking about, telling himself that at a time like this it was necessary to think about something more than the weather but nothing to do with sex and it was a matter of finding the right thing between those two subjects that would take him out of the waiting and far from Angela. He wanted something to give him a lift. Despite his initial resolve to keep away from the subject of sex but knowing it would take him away from the desk and the phone he started on the topic of women.

At first it was women in general because no one face came to mind, it was all women in every shape and size, and everything he found attractive in them, their voices, necks and ears, their legs with muscles showing when they walked, their stomachs and thighs and arms when they wore very little to cover themselves up, every detail he could manage to think of until slowly all the women formed themselves into one woman, and it was Angela, and then he was feeling very low again.

He folded his arms on the desk, let his head rest against his arms, closed his eyes to the knowledge that life listed him as hooked and helpless and just another morsel to be chewed by bigger fish or swallowed whole with very little fuss.

Then he was thinking how this city that didn't rank as high in the same field of perversity as others still had its particular form of magnetism and sorcery that drew the people who lived in it out of their routine and into excess until all they wanted was more until more wasn't enough. He accepted the fact that he wasn't different from any of them when he met Angela and knew that he wouldn't stop chasing her until he got her and that when he did have her it certainly wouldn't be enough to satisfy him. None of that kept him from wanting more.

But he wasn't anywhere near a result that might begin to satisfy him and he figured he might never see Angela again and if he did see her he wasn't so sure she'd be interested in him since he didn't have the slightest idea what made her tick. He told himself all of this like someone wrapped in a wet blanket talking to the world. He was still feeling very low. He stood up, paced the room, lit a cigarette and sat down at the desk again. He drummed his fingers on the desk.

The telephone rang. It was ten fifty-five. He listened to the voice on the other end of the line but didn't register the words until after he'd put the phone down. He hadn't said a word, just listened to Violet Archer who said she was at home and wanted to talk to him right away, it was urgent, she couldn't wait, she'd be right over and it didn't matter if he was undressed and in bed because that was where she wanted him.

He shook his head wondering how she'd got his number. She wasn't drunk, her voice was clear and the things she'd said were organized into a plan and he couldn't figure out what that plan was except that he knew that he was right in the middle of it. He swept the cigarette ash off the desk in front of him.

The telephone rang again at fifteen minutes past eleven. It was Shimura.

"I've got good news," he said.
"Don't tell me."
"You want to know, don't you?"
"I don't think I can take any news, good or bad."
"Sure you can. She's coming home."

[*71*]

The following morning at nine-thirty Shimura phoned Rand Hadley
from the agency to let him know how things stood in the case of the so-
called kidnapping of Angela Mason, which was drawing to a close more
smoothly and easily than he'd anticipated now with Fitch's complete
cooperation and no pressure on the financial end from Kawamura,
who'd given him a free hand.

"I can't say which part satisfies me more, Kawamura's trust or a
problem on the verge of resolution," Shimura said.

"How's Pohl taking it?"

"Nervous as a cat."

"Can you do anything for him?"

"No, he's got to play the cards as they're dealt him. I'll be around
when he needs me, you know that, Rand."

"Of course you will. Have you got the place staked out?"

"There isn't much left to do. Eto's watching the house. I'm waiting
for a call from Fitch."

"By this time tomorrow she'll be tucked safely in her own bed.
And you can get a good night's sleep knowing you've done everything
possible to help a friend and there's nothing like that feeling to give us
a boost when there isn't always a lot going our way on the order of
satisfaction on the job."

"I don't like to hear that coming from you. You had a lot of good
years with the county. When you were lead investigator there were
arrests and convictions. But maybe there's something you're trying to
tell me."

"I don't have any complaints," Hadley said, scribbling the letter *v*
with a circle around it, then *s* with a circle around it on a notepad in
front of him. "The guys upstairs gave me a pat on the back plenty of
times. I got promotions, acknowledgment from the detectives I worked

with, and the victims who made it out of a tough spot because of the department thanked me more often in twenty-five years than I can remember, but there's nothing like the feeling of having done something for the best reason in the world."

"And what's that?"

"When whatever it is that makes us tick tells us to go ahead and do something right for somebody even if it isn't by the book, like you've done for Pohl, knowing it might not go down the right way with the people upstairs."

"Noble principles, Rand—like how things ought to be instead of how they are. After all the years with the county you know that."

"And you know I'm right or you wouldn't have stuck your neck out for him."

72

It was three forty-five in the afternoon when Fitch gave Shimura a call. He was going to Nightingale Lane to give Angela a drug to knock her out and then hand her over to Shimura if he was ready to take the responsibility for her, which was more than Fitch said he was willing to do because he'd had enough of playing out of his league with a nutcase.

"I'll take the responsibility all right," Shimura said. "What time should I be there?"

"Number four at five-thirty."

Shimura put the phone down, looked at his wristwatch.

Aoyama came to his office five minutes later. Shimura pointed to a chair, Aoyama sat down, crossed his legs, offered Shimura a cigarette.

"No, thanks."

Aoyama lit his cigarette, then sat up straight.

They sat there for some moments, not saying anything, just looking at the short distance of space between them.

Shimura smiled at Aoyama.

"Well," he said. "Let's wrap it up."

"When do we leave?"

"Forty-five minutes."

Aoyama took a deep breath, thought for a moment, then said: "What about Fitch? Can we count on him?"

"Of course, we can. He's had enough of it to last him a lifetime." Shimura pulled his chair close to the desk. "And he's honest."

"Quit kidding."

"I'm serious. He's one of the few left who've got a sense of honor. I told you what he told me last night."

"Keep telling me."

"If you can't buy it—"

"I'm buying it," Aoyama said.

"Good. You know where Eto is, don't you?"

"On stake-out. I'm not babysitting Eto."

"I know that. What's eating you?"

"Sorry. It's Eto." He took a hard pull at the cigarette. "His bank account is low and he's worried and he doesn't know how to straighten it out."

Shimura's expression became solemn. "He's gambling, and losing."

"Of course he's gambling."

"You introduced him to it."

"Maybe I did, but I do it to pass the time, and he does it because he's got to do it."

"His father was a gambler. Maybe not in casinos, but he lost plenty of money."

Aoyama put his cigarette out, lit another.

"So what's the difference between him and his father?"

"Don't ask stupid questions," Aoyama said. "You know as well as I do that they're the same man, father and son, and it's only the difference in age that separates them."

"That's right, but I'd like to help him."

"I know, but he can't change overnight."

"Don't make excuses for him."

"I'm not making excuses for anybody."

"And I'm not talking about twenty-four hours," Shimura said. "It's a long time that he's been doing the same thing one way or another and I thought he wanted to quit and he's in it now just as deep as he was then."

"I'm not babysitting Eto," Aoyama insisted.

"I didn't say you were."

"Okay."

"You said it."

"How's that?"

"He's got you in a lousy mood, again."

"What's that got to do with it?"

"Think about it."

"Okay, I'm sorry. I just wish he'd lay off me."

"Why don't you tell him?"

"He doesn't want to hear it. And he owes me money. I can't piss him off because he won't pay me back if he's pissed off."

"Then tell me this. Did you have to loan it to him?"

Aoyama blinked several times. "Let's see, now — " He frowned up at the ceiling, then looked at Shimura. "Let's not go into it, okay?"

"You're trying to help him the wrong way, then you get fucked up by it," Shimura said mildly.

"Give me a break, will you?"

Shimura leaned back in his chair.

"Now tell me this," he said. "What's the difference between you and him?"

Aoyama took another drag at his cigarette.

"I give up," he said.

"This thing with the money is just an idea you got, but it's not a very good idea. It's more like an excuse for getting yourself stuck in a problem."

Aoyama shook his head, frowning thoughtfully.

"You can't help everybody out of everything they get themselves mixed up in," Shimura said.

It was just like every other time Shimura had sat him down for a few words meant to straighten him out and Aoyama had listened to what he had to say and knew that Shimura was right and that he'd got himself into a fucked-up situation, and so he felt a bit stupid and embarrassed and at the same time grateful that Shimura was telling him to watch his step because he told him in a way that meant it mattered to Shimura what happened to him.

Aoyama stared at the floor. Finally he looked up, nodded slowly, and mumbled: "What do you think?"

"That we get into the car and go over to 4 Nightingale Lane."

73

Pohl put on a clean pair of underwear and socks, a laundered shirt, jeans, then polished shoes. He combed his half-white hair in front of the bathroom mirror. His face looked back at him and gave him a guilty smile. It was eleven forty-five. Violet would be pressing the buzzer in a couple of minutes.

He didn't know why he'd given Violet his address, he didn't have any expectations and didn't want anything from her, but it wasn't just curiosity about what she'd have to say that made him feel the way he was feeling now. He tried to tell himself the reason was certainly some unknown reason, but he knew he was kidding himself.

He began to ask himself some questions and pretty soon he got the answers and didn't like them because it added up to two very important things, the first thing being that he'd taken a good look at his own eager face in the mirror, and the second was the promise of Angela's homecoming that'd given his mind a twist—he was remembering the game with the vibrator and ball-gag—and so he had to admit he was thinking only about sex, no matter how much he scratched the itch never went away, and then he heard the buzzer.

He opened the door. Violet was standing there looking at him with her green eyes and black hair and a grin that told him he'd better watch out because he was about to get swallowed up whole. She wore a khaki knee-length raincoat and a knee-length skirt and a short-sleeved sweater, her legs were bare, she wore low-heeled shoes.

"Are you going to make me stand out here?" she said. "You can look at me all you want when I'm inside."

His eyes were wide. He gaped at her.

"You going to let me in?" she repeated. "I'd sure like to come in."

He took a very deep breath. He looked at the open door and then his gaze went over to Violet, going up the length of her from the shoes to the jet-black hair. He stepped aside to let her in. She brushed against him, he smelled a faint flammable odor, and he remembered that it was her natural scent. He shut the door behind her, locked it.

She went straight to the living room like she already knew the layout and took off her raincoat, folding it over the back of a chair. She spun around to face him and her skirt twirled with the motion. Pohl didn't want to shut his eyes, it was just a reflex. They were shut, and when he realized they were shut he opened them right away to get a look at her.

"Okay, you want me to do it again?" she said, spinning to show him what she was wearing under her skirt.

He looked her up and down again. She caught a glimpse of a bulge in his crotch.

"We're going to have a little talk," she said. "You got anything to drink?"

Pohl was moving calmly toward her with a measured stride. He didn't want her to know he had to catch his breath. "What would you like?"

"Vodka," she said.

"No vodka."

"What have you got?"

"What's it look like?" he flipped back at her. "A hard-on."

"And what's wrong with that?"

"Whisky and soda, okay?"

"Whisky and soda it is."

He turned around, his face red, and went to the kitchen to make a couple of drinks and to cool down. He came back with them and saw she was sitting in an armchair with her legs crossed, wagging her foot at him. He gave her the drink. He felt the temperature of his skin climb again.

She saw it, smiled, and took a sip from her glass.

"You don't know me and I don't know you but I've been thinking about you since the other night," she said.

"I haven't been thinking of you," he said gently, trying to protect himself.

"Maybe not. But here I am."

He couldn't argue the point, so he sat down in a chair opposite her with his drink in his hand and waited for her to say more.

Violet said nothing. She looked at him, took another sip from her glass. Her foot kept on wagging at him.

He was in for something he'd wanted for a long time but didn't have the guts to get for himself because he was passive and it would have to come to him if he was going to get it. He wanted a release valve to let off steam and the steam was his frustration with Angela, and it looked as if something that had come out of left field, Violet Archer, was going to ease that pressure. It was a normal buildup of the kind of thing that happens to a man who hasn't been with a woman in a long time and it had to be taken care of right away.

What he couldn't figure out was why it was going to happen the very night before Angela came back. If Violet said she wanted to fuck him, he didn't know if he'd say yes or no because of Angela, and it was on the order of a quiz show and it worried him that maybe he wouldn't have the right answer.

"What are we going to talk about?" he asked.

She leaned forward and said: "You and me." She finished her drink in a gulp. "For instance, what do we have in common?"

"I don't know you." Pohl tried to make it sound casual.

"You don't have to know me to know what I want."

"What have you got in mind?"

"Plenty." She stared at him, uncrossed her legs and opened them to give him a view.

Pohl nearly choked on his drink.

"Usually I talk about money at this point, but I'm tired of it," she said. "Come here, on your knees."

Pohl didn't get what she meant about money but he followed instructions and crawled toward her until his head was between her legs.

"Lick me."

She took a handful of his hair and pulled his mouth against the crotch of her panties and he stuck his tongue out and got them wet and then pulled at the material with his teeth. After a minute he felt a couple of fingers against his upper lip trying to get past his mouth and when they did get where they were going they pulled the piece of fabric aside and he had access to where he wanted to go.

When he came up for air, his eyes focused on the soft skin between her legs and he saw the glistening wetness of where he'd been and a scar that was a blemish on her inner thigh. He touched it with his index finger, then slipped two fingers inside her, spread the fingers and moved them rapidly in and out while the heel of his other hand pressed down on her lower belly.

A transparent liquid came out of her, a low sound came from the back of her throat, and he moved his hand faster until his wrist was soaked.

Violet looked at him through crossed eyes and when they uncrossed and she saw him clearly she was looking at a cracked smile on his face that made him look like he was high as a kite. Pohl sat back on his folded legs. He wore a grin and at the corners of it there was plenty of saliva.

"This gets very interesting," she said.

Pohl wiped his mouth, smiled amiably, aiming the smile at the very wet place between her legs, then bringing it up along her flat belly and crumpled skirt and sending the smile past the short-sleeved sweater, driving it farther on and finally parking it on her full lips. Her green eyes burnt a hole in his forehead and he started to sweat.

74

Fitch wasn't used to going to 4 Nightingale Lane in daylight. He wasn't used to doing much in daylight because he was either asleep or planning another job at the earliest in the late afternoon, and now he felt as if everyone was watching him as he drove past them on a busy street. But he shrugged it off, he was tired, and gave himself a smile and his eyes shimmered. He was almost through with trying to figure out and fend off Angela Mason. He switched on the radio.

The afternoon sun shone yellowish-orange across the hood of the car. He looked through the windshield at the passing shops, a nursery of plants and trees and a gas station on his left, went through the green light, and then suddenly the smile faded from his face as he rubbed a thumbnail lightly across his underlip.

What'll I do when I've finished the thing I've been doing every night with Angela? But there were a lot of messages on his answering machine and he told himself that he had plenty of things to do with a dozen calls and more clients than that waiting for him to come around out of this job and make himself available for the next one. You get what I'm saying? There isn't anything to worry about so quit worrying.

His eyes were on the road but he wasn't concentrating and a truck with a tarp tied down over the bed cut in front of him and he swerved and leaned hard on the horn. The truck turned right at the next intersection.

"Fuck," he said with his head inclined and his eyes narrowed. Without sound he said, You sure that's what you figure on doing?

But he didn't have an answer because he was busy looking for the turn onto Hartrey and when he found it he took the turn and continued to the end of Hartrey and made a left, following the drive a short distance until he got to Delaplaine Road, then turned right and went straight to Lavergne Terrace. He pulled over to the curb in front of the garden at the center of Lavergne Terrace, shut off the engine. Fitch was two blocks away from the small, four-room house at 4 Nightingale Lane in Pigsville.

The sun was going down slowly. He sat behind the wheel contemplating the change of light, then reached over to the glove compartment and removed a special sack that kept its contents cold. He took a narrow, rectangular box out of the sack that held his personal set of chloral hydrate suppositories, individually sealed in a foil jacket, shaped like bullets. He'd put them in the box with its padded cradles before he left his apartment. Each suppository of the brand Aquachloral was 650mg. The right dose would take effect in about half an hour, which meant giving her two of them, inducing sleep in less than an hour. Their melting point was 135°F. He snapped the case shut and reached into his shirt pocket for a cigarette.

He thought of the moment he would put them inside Angela and smiled because he was an ordinary man and it was a real pleasure to see himself spreading the cheeks of her ass. He knew the instructions by heart:

> *If the suppository is too soft to insert, chill it in the refrigerator for 30 minutes or run cold water over it before removing the foil wrapper.*
>
> *To insert suppository — First remove the foil wrapper and moisten the suppository with cold water. Lie down on your left side and raise your right knee to your chest. (A left-handed person should lie on the right side and raise the left knee.) Using your finger, insert the suppository into the rectum, about ½ to 1 inch in infants and children and 1 inch in adults. Hold it in place for a few moments.*
>
> *Stand up after about 15 minutes. Wash your hands thoroughly and resume your normal activities.*
>
> *For rectal dosage form (suppositories):*
>
> *For trouble in sleeping: Adults — 500 to 1000 mg at bedtime.*

Fitch put the box in the side pocket of his jacket, got out of the car and locked the door. He walked toward Nightingale Lane without a hardcover notebook, smoking and avoiding garbage strewn along the sidewalk and listening to the birds singing in the overhanging branches of trees. He came to the four-room wooden house at 4 Nightingale Lane and went around to the back and let himself in.

Angela wasn't expecting him. She didn't know whether or not it was daylight but she had developed an internal clock that told her Fitch was a lot earlier than usual. He took off her blindfold and untied her arms and legs and she rubbed the irritated places where the rope had rubbed against her skin. She was barefoot and there were red marks around her ankles. Fitch tossed his cigarette in the toilet, flushed it down.

"We're finished," he said matter-of-factly.

"I knew that already."

"I'm going to give you something to put you out," he said. "Then I'll take you home."

"You'll get paid. I'll give you cash."

"It's not the money I'm worried about. I know you're good for it. But I want to talk to you about life after therapy." He emphasized the last words with a bit too much sarcasm to make her understand that he was worn out by the whole thing and had something else on his mind.

"What kind of crack is that?"

"Listen, I don't want you to tell anybody about what we've been doing." He was staring at her and feeling uneasy and not knowing why. "You got it?"

"What difference does it make?"

"It's not good for my reputation."

"Okay, I got it."

Fitch took the box out of his jacket pocket, laid it on the back of the toilet, swung around and said: "Maybe you should use the toilet. It's not going to be an injection."

She understood him. "Maybe you should leave the room."

"I'll be right here." He went out with the box in his hand, leaving the door ajar.

"Of course you'll be right here. You wouldn't miss this for the world."

Fitch winced, leaned against the wall opposite the door, lit a cigarette.

She unbuttoned her jeans, sat on the toilet seat, her head down and hands at the side of her head with her fingers wound into her hair, then she fingered the diamond in her navel.

Fitch listened to her emptying her bowels to make way for the chloral hydrate suppositories. He had a lot of respect for her, and because it was Angela Mason doing it he didn't think twice about what he was hearing hit the water in the toilet bowl. The toilet flushed. He knocked at the door and went in. He was finished with his cigarette.

"I'm done," she said, buttoning her jeans.

"Don't do that."

He dropped his cigarette in the toilet, put the cover down but didn't flush it.

"What?"

"We might as well get down to it right now."

"Okay, what do you want me to do?"

"Pull your pants all the way down, your underwear, too, and lie here" — he pointed at the floor — "on your side, raise your leg and bring the knee up to your chest."

"You're a pro."

"Cut it out."

He opened the box, removed two suppositories and unwrapped one of them, threw the foil in the wastebasket, and put the suppository under the running faucet for a second before bending down on one knee and letting himself admire her narrow hips and small, rounded ass.

She turned her head to look at him. "Keep your mind on your work," she said grimly.

"Don't get excited." Fitch put his index finger in his mouth, got it very wet and gently rubbed the saliva-soaked tip of his finger around her anus.

"Hey, what're you doing?"

He started to laugh, it built itself up into a big laugh and he couldn't control himself because now he was shaking with laughter until he began to lose his balance, and then he felt a heavy blow to the side of his head that came from the open palm of her hand. It was strong enough to knock him over.

Fitch's head struck the base of the toilet, he slumped to the floor and lost consciousness. Angela got to her feet with her pants around her ankles. She propped herself up using both hands on the edge of the sink. She pulled her panties up, then the jeans, and buttoned them. She ran water from the faucet and washed her face and let the water run down her chin and didn't dry herself off.

Angela bent down and looked at Fitch's wristwatch. It was almost four-thirty. She started to leave the bathroom and got one foot into the hallway before she laughed to herself and the laughing went on as she turned around. She crouched next to him, unbuttoned and unzipped his trousers and tugged them slowly down the length of his inert legs until they were around his ankles with one knee awkwardly bent over the other leg. She pulled down his underwear and saw his hairy ass cheeks. She made an effort not to burst out laughing at what she was about to do.

The suppository he'd been holding in his hand before she'd knocked him down was on the floor just beyond his fingertips and she reached down to pick it up, ran cold water in the sink to moisten it, and then bent down again to the job at hand. She spread his ass cheeks with one hand and with the other inserted the suppository an inch into his rectum. She ran cold water over another suppository, unwrapped it, moistened it and put it inside him like she was loading a shotgun.

With some effort, because she wasn't used to exerting herself, she pulled up his underwear and then his trousers, zipped and buttoned them. He lay on the floor, breathing slowly. She patted him on the ass.

Angela washed her hands with the old piece of soap beside the faucet and wiped them dry on her jeans. She looked down at Fitch, shook her head, left the bathroom for the hallway, the kitchen, and then she used the rear exit to get out of 4 Nightingale Lane.

She'd forgot to look for her shoes, they weren't on her feet when she looked down at them, so she made her way barefoot through the small backyard past crumpled newspapers and greasy plastic containers, climbed a low fence and got herself moving on the sidewalk that ran along the street a block away and parallel to Nightingale Lane bathed in the last yellowish-orange glow of the sun on the horizon. The ground felt cool and soothing on the soles of her feet.

She walked along not looking where she was going and thinking instead about what it meant to want to fall in love and trying to add it up. And what it amounted to was that for her love was a pain in the ass, and it wasn't a solution to anything because in her opinion a source of suffering wasn't a solution, and that was it, she got the idea to have herself kidnapped just to figure out a thing that's better off left alone because if she went on chasing after it without really believing in its importance she'd lose her mind.

She'd just go on living the way she'd been living without trying anything new that would only end up squeezing the inspiration out of her like shoes that were too small for her feet. Then she stepped on a small stone and hopped up and down in pain. She couldn't bring herself to smile. She rubbed the bottom of her foot, then went to the corner and turned without thinking where she was going, knowing she was going somewhere in a hurry.

Her eyes were partially closed and the glow of the setting sun was blurred. She had enough change in her pocket to take the bus. She waited at a bus stop for fifteen minutes, a bus arrived, and then she was taking it to a stop near the river. She got off at the intersection of Winthrop and Front Street, and she kept on going at a careful pace away from the river, avoiding cigarette butts, discarded beer cans and puddles of urine on the sidewalk.

She walked until she got to Jackson. She continued on Jackson Street, and then to Fourteenth Street, and saw a battered red car parked in front of Burt Pohl's apartment building. She stepped around broken glass from a smashed bottle of cheap wine and went up to the entrance to ring the buzzer.

She'd thought of Pohl while she'd had only time to think when she was tied up between sessions with Fitch, and she decided because of Pohl's patience with her that he was the only man she could trust to have a useful conversation about what had happened with her plan to have herself kidnapped and kept away from the world and to follow a particular kind of therapy she'd invented with Fitch.

She pressed the button on the intercom. She waited for a voice to speak to her. She pressed the button again. She raised each leg one leg at a time to look at the filthy soles of her feet. The sky showed its twilight, there was a faint breeze that blew against her flushed cheeks. For the first time in several hours, she noticed she was hungry.

"Who is it?" Pohl's voice crackled through the speaker at her.

"Me, Angela."

There was a long silence.

The front door buzzed to let her in.

75

Shimura sat with Aoyama in the car parked beneath the branches of a tree on Lavergne Terrace, either watching the clock on the dashboard or staring blankly at the small garden opposite them. Eto had gone home. It was five-fifteen. There were at least six cigarette butts on the ground outside Aoyama's window on the passenger side of the car. Shimura didn't feel like smoking. The sky was the color of burnt orange with streaks of red reaching through it like faraway clouds.

"What do you think? Will he bring her out?" Aoyama said, looking down at his shoes.

"Of course he'll bring her out."

Fitch's car was parked nearby in front of the garden.

"When?"

"We've got fifteen minutes. If he doesn't come out with her in fifteen minutes we go in."

"Okay." He lit another cigarette.

"It's going to kill you."

"What is?"

"Smoking like that."

Aoyama didn't answer him, he stared out the window. One-story four-room wooden houses that weren't in such a bad state as the houses on Nightingale Lane stared back at him. Every now and then someone came out of a house to walk a dog, collect mail and a newspaper from a mailbox or stand on the porch and gaze up at the sky.

"It's a sad place, Pigsville," Aoyama observed, throwing his cigarette out the window.

It was five-thirty.

"Maybe it is, maybe it isn't," Shimura said. "Let's go." He got out of the car, waited for Aoyama to do the same, locked his door, then locked the door on the passenger side.

When they got to 4 Nightingale Lane they automatically went around the house to the back because making an entrance at the front door was out of character for them, and they always followed the guidelines of the Kawamura Agency. Shimura yawned before he grasped the door handle, he hadn't slept very well the night before with Tomiko in town. Aoyama thought he was professionally dispassionate.

The back door wasn't locked. Shimura gave it a gentle shove with his shoulder and pushed it all the way open with his foot. They went into the house, smelled the stale air, passed through the kitchen and into the hallway. A faint light sprayed out from the bathroom. It was the only light on in the house.

Shimura stood in front of Aoyama who peered over his shoulder at the bathroom door, looking down at the figure of Fitch sprawled on the floor unconscious or sound sleep. His feet in their polished shoes were pointing awkwardly south.

76

Angela didn't wait for the elevator, she climbed the stairs slowly, feeling the smooth, worn-out carpet beneath her bare feet.

After Pohl let her into the building, he hurried to the bathroom to get dressed, tripped over a pair of shoes, and fumbled nervously with his clothes. He put on a T-shirt, buttoned his jeans. He had forgot that Violet was in his bed until he heard her voice shout at him from the bedroom.

"Who was it?" she said, her head propped up by a couple of pillows.

"What?"

"Who was at the door?"

"Nobody." He straightened his hair in front of the mirror. "Fuck," he said to himself. He searched the hamper for a pair of socks.

"What?"

"Nothing, please," he pleaded. "I've got to get dressed."

"What's the matter with you?"

"I told you, nothing."

"That's exactly what you've told me—nothing."

"Leave me the fuck alone."

It just came out without prior consideration and Pohl was sorry the minute he'd heard himself say it.

"What did you say to me?"

Before he could answer her, Violet was out of bed and walking quickly on bare feet out of the bedroom and into the bathroom, and if she'd been wearing something she would've been rolling up her sleeves, but she wasn't wearing anything, just her supple body marching toward him on strong slender legs, her nipples hard because they were out in the air from beneath the bedcovers, her hands clenched into fists ready for a fight.

A sock dropped from Pohl's hand when he saw her coming. He hopped backward in the direction of the bathtub on the foot with a sock already on it while Violet advanced until she was standing right in front of him. He tripped, and he was falling backward through the shower curtain into the bathtub when she caught him by the wrists and pulled him out and upright.

"So much for your acrobatic skills," she said with her teeth clenched.

"Yeah, thanks."

"Don't thank me, just don't talk to me like that."

She'd got herself into the same act and rhythm as Burnett had used when he played with her, and she liked it.

"Tough, aren't you?" Pohl said.

He grabbed her bare shoulders and kissed her on the mouth. The doorbell rang. He searched the floor for the sock he'd dropped, found it, put it on and went to answer the door. Violet walked back to bed with her hips swaying only a little because she figured he wasn't watching her.

Pohl unlocked the door, opened it as far as the chain allowed, and saw Angela standing in front of him with a tired expression on her face, out of breath from climbing the stairs. He shut the door on her, heard her mild voice say his name, then unhooked the chain to let her in. Even barefoot, she was a couple of inches taller than Pohl. She walked past him into the living room.

Pohl shut the door, locked it. He followed Angela into the living room. She looked around at everything in the room as if she'd never seen it before.

"You've been here a dozen times. What are you looking at?"

"Nothing. Something's changed," she said.

"Nothing's changed." He almost choked on what he'd said.

"Well, I want to talk to you about what's been going on."

"You're worn out. Why don't you sit down?"

She sat down in an armchair, stretched her legs out in front of her. "I'm thirsty."

"What do you want to drink?"

"Water. A glass of water with plenty of ice."

Pohl went into the kitchen. Angela stared at her feet, wiggled her toes, and saw the filth between them that came from walking barefoot on the street.

Pohl gave her a tall glass of ice water. She drank it down in one gulp.

"I've got to wash my feet, they're disgusting."

"You can use the tub."

She stood up and gave the glass back to him.

"I'll need a wash cloth."

Pohl led the way to the bathroom, she followed him. He handed her a clean towel from the towel rack next to the sink.

"You can leave me alone, I'll be right out." She shut the bathroom door.

Pohl stood facing the door, scratched his head, coughed, thought of having a cigarette, then remembered Violet. The bedroom door was ajar, he opened it and went in. Violet was snug under the covers with her black hair spread out behind her head, resting on three white pillows. She held a magazine open in her hands, turning the pages slowly.

"Well, who is it?" she said, without looking up at him.

"A woman I've known for a long time."

"You mean a girlfriend?"

"Not exactly."

"An ex-girlfriend?"

"No."

"What then?" She set the magazine down beside her and pulled the covers up to her chin.

"I can't exactly say."

"Why can't you exactly say?" She imitated his voice. "What do you think I'm going to do, scratch your eyes out or something like in the movies? I've been around the block."

"I'm sure you have."

"What kind of remark is that?"

"Nothing, I didn't mean anything."

"I'm beginning to think you never mean anything you say."

Pohl sat down on the edge of the bed, next to her.

"Listen, Violet—" He reached out and stroked her silky hair.

"Quit playing lovesick adolescent and tell me what's on your mind."

"You're impossible, that's what's on my mind."

"And don't forget that's exactly why you want to fuck me."

She pulled him toward her, let him kiss her, then drew back the covers to give him a place in bed and the magazine fell to the floor. She ruffled his hair, he moved closer to her and sniffed her skin, kissed her lips and neck, then he buried his face between her breasts and began sucking her nipple.

She suddenly felt a tingling sensation in her body that wasn't familiar and which she didn't understand because maybe this was starting to feel like the kind of sex she didn't think existed on earth, and maybe she was falling in love.

She wondered if it was a kind of brainwashing, and then decided that whether or not it was brainwashing she didn't care. She pulled the T-shirt over his head and tossed it past the side of the bed, dragged him under the covers, unbuttoning his jeans and biting him.

While he was thinking that this might just turn out to be something on the order of what Shimura had said Kawamura and Asami had together, a kind of true love, but their own particular version of it, she was busy with what she knew how to do, which was wrapping her lips around his cock and swallowing him until his pubic hair tickled her nose. He smiled, his face hurt because it was a hard, broad smile that nearly shut his eyes and he didn't know if it was going to make him laugh or cry.

They didn't hear Angela come into the room. They were listening to something else, and it was something on the order of two people holding hands swimming deep underwater against the current without the drag of the effort and paying attention only to the very important sound of blood pounding in their ears that came from a pair of like-minded hearts.

Angela was barefoot and the door was open and all she had to do was walk in because it was as if Pohl and Violet were saying: "Come on in the water's fine," when in fact they weren't saying anything at all because they were too busy fucking.

And while she was standing in the doorway looking at Pohl tangled in bed with a woman she didn't know and had never seen before, she thought about how she'd always taken for granted that he loved her and that he'd always love her and that she'd used that love like she did with every other man she'd known, and here he was with somebody else, so instead of talking to him about what she'd had in mind, the point of love in her life, or the pointlessness of it, a topic there was no longer any need to waste time talking about, she took off her clothes and got into bed with them.

The mattress suddenly weighed more than it had a few seconds ago and the downward slant it took was enough to make Pohl and Violet turn their heads and see Angela climbing in for some of the action.

Violet gave Pohl a little shove with her warm hands, Pohl pulled himself out of her, dropped gently alongside her lean body, bent his elbow and the palm of his hand propped his head up while Angela, perched above them on her knees on the other side of Violet, hands flat on the bed sheet, looked them both up and down. Violet was shaking, she was angry.

"No matter how many lovers a woman has there's always one she can't bear to lose to another woman," Angela said, winking at Violet.

Violet's face was flushed, she'd heard that line before. She said: "Who's she? And what the fuck is she doing here?"

Pohl didn't have an answer for her, and since he couldn't find anything to say it told him that he didn't know what to do and the fact that he didn't know what to do seemed to inform him there was a big problem here. He sat up and stared at Angela. A pulse beat in her throat. She was so beautiful he wanted to shut his eyes.

There was love that had everything to do with fucking, and there was another kind of love and fucking was part of it, and it was that other kind of love he felt for Angela Mason, a love that no matter how hard he tried he'd never get away from it because it was something that had burned and burrowed into him and it went deeper than logic and was on the order of a permanent fire working its way from the inside out.

"You better go," he said, looking at Violet.

Violet sat straight up in bed, her hair fell across her face, she caught a few strands with her fingertips and put them in her mouth, ignored Angela, clenched her fists, and her slanted green eyes looked searchingly at Pohl. Angela rocked backward and pushed herself off the bed, found an armchair and sat in it with her legs crossed, waving her bare foot at the scene on the bed.

"Do you mean it?"

"Yes, I'm sorry."

"Do you know what you're saying?"

"Now more than ever."

"You're an asshole."

"Maybe. Probably."

"I thought—"

"Please, don't think. Just get out of bed and get dressed. It's the right thing to do. Trust me."

"Trust you?"

"Okay, don't trust me. It's not important. Good-bye."

"Yes, good-bye," Angela said from the armchair.

"You've got change coming," Violet said, without looking at Angela, and she slapped Pohl hard on the face.

"You have every right—"

"Don't talk about rights," Violet said, climbing out of bed, gathering her clothes in her arms. She felt two pairs of eyes give her a shove out of the room.

The apartment door slammed shut, they were alone. Pohl reached for the bed sheets to cover his embarrassment, but the embarrassment went a lot further than his nakedness because he didn't know how to handle the situation now that he'd got rid of Violet Archer. He'd been waiting a long time for an opportunity to see Angela, and the opportunity had come and he felt the weight and size of it on his shoulders, and it was a weight that came from the fact that he'd been wanting her for what seemed like a lifetime, and the size of it was on the order of something very big because here she was without any clothes on, sitting in a chair with her right foot waving at him, telling him to come up with something good or she'd disappear again.

He thought of how badly he'd wanted to see her, and he remembered how happy he thought he'd be when finally she was sitting with him in some restaurant or bar and they were talking, and when they were talking they'd be having a conversation about nothing and everything because nothing and everything meant something to them, and laughing, too, it was important that they'd be laughing, and then he'd know that something on the order of intimacy was getting under way between them. And so he used this particular memory to give him courage.

Now he was pretty sure it was going to be all right, and it was easier to breathe, easier to think. The whole thing was leaning toward his side of it. It was going along with him. Everything and everybody was going along, and what he told himself now was that even if he didn't know the reason why she was here at least he knew that she wanted to be alone with him, she had something to say or do that had to be said or done between the two of them alone. The surprise he'd felt at first was wearing off, he wasn't completely in the clear, but now he knew what he was going to do about it. He stared at Angela but she wasn't looking at him. Her sea-blue eyes were darting around the room, studying it.

"This place needs some straightening up," she said. "You ought to keep things neater in here."

And everything positive he'd been feeling a minute ago collapsed in a heap on the floor and he went down into a black pit and he couldn't feel a thing.

"You don't have to tell me that," he said, looking away from her at the disorder in the room.

He tried to climb out of the hole, got his head a few inches above it, saying: "Don't you have something you want to tell me?"

"There are a lot things I'd like to tell you, but you wouldn't understand."

"Try me. I might not understand, but I'd like to know anyway."

"How long have you been living here?"

"Oh, Jesus — you know how long I've been living here."

"I shouldn't have come."

"What is it, Angela? Why don't you talk to me?"

"I wish I could tell you, but I can't."

"Why can't you? What's wrong with talking about it?"

"Because there's no point in it now. And there probably wasn't a point in it when I did what I'd done in the first place. At the beginning. That's what I've learned. But it doesn't matter. Nothing like that matters now. You believe me, don't you?"

"I don't follow you."

"You can't understand what you know nothing about."

"That's an awfully big thing to say. Try telling it some other way. I just threw another woman out of here."

"I didn't mean it to be cruel. That's one thing. And the other thing is that what you did to her, you *had* to do."

"And you *know* I had to do it."

"Now who's being cruel?"

"Come here. Sit down next to me." He gestured toward the bed, patted it with the palm of his hand.

She didn't move from the chair but her foot kept on wagging at him.

"I'm all right where I am," she said. It was under a whisper.

"Maybe you are, maybe you aren't."

He sounded confident again, he knew that, but he knew too that there was a look of hard-up desire written all over his face, and that it kept her where she was, away from him and still in the room, but away from him.

The flames inside working their way out finally reached the surface and scorched him. He was suffering because of it, and he had to do something right away, move around, get out of bed and move around the room to take away the discomfort because it was really hurting him and he was going to get eaten up by the flames.

Pohl tugged at the bed sheets, pulled them out from under the blanket while keeping part of them wrapped around his waist to protect him from showing his weakness, then tried to drag himself out of bed, out of the twisted up mess he'd made of his bed, the thing he'd got himself tangled up in now, and the whole mess he'd made of his life and the time spent waiting for Angela Mason. She was something he really wanted and if she'd only work along with him it might go somewhere, but it wasn't going to go anywhere, she wasn't going to go anywhere with him, and nothing could make her do that since she herself wasn't made for doing it.

He wanted to blame her, it would've been an easy thing to do, but he couldn't blame her for something she hadn't done to him. He wanted to hate her, and that would've been just as easy to do as blaming her for what had happened because he could hate her for everything she'd put him through, but the truth was that he hated himself and blamed himself for wanting her so much that the flames he felt now were busy taking away the best part of him and leaving him with nothing.

He tripped over the bed sheets and fell backward but caught himself by taking hold of the dresser. The sheets still covered him up and there was nothing to be ashamed of and he was standing on his own two feet, so his eyes focused on Angela gathering her clothes from the floor in front of the doorway and getting into them item by item, and while it might've been a pleasure under other circumstances to watch her getting dressed, the situation wasn't at all what he'd wanted or hoped it would be, she didn't once look up to see what he was doing or how he felt about what she was doing, she was busy getting ready to leave him.

They might've said good-bye, Burt Pohl couldn't remember whether or not they'd said anything, it was such a long time ago, it seemed like forever, but he stood at the window anyway and looked out at the street and saw Angela Mason walking barefoot along Fourteenth Street away from the apartment building and the battered red car and out of his life with the air of a woman who knew who she was and where she was going.

About the Author

Born in Milwaukee, Wisconsin, Mark Fishman has lived and worked in Paris since 1995. His short stories have appeared in a number of literary reviews such as the *Carolina Quarterly,* the *Chicago Review,* the *Mississippi Review, The Literary Review,* and *Glimmer Train. No. 22 Pleasure City* is Mark's second novel. His first, *The Magic Dogs of San Vicente,* was published by Guernica Editions in 2016.

Printed in May 2018
by Gauvin Press,
Gatineau, Québec